Solix

Resettles Blue Mountain

by
Robert E. Dansby

Photographs by
Daniel J. Cox

Edgenics Media

Solix Resettles Blue Mountain
Copyright © 2006 by Robert E. Dansby
Photographs Copyright © 2006 by Daniel J. Cox
Book Design by: Robert E. Dansby
Edited by: Diana Bloom
Cover Design by: Beth McKain

Library of Congress Control Number: 2006909929
Library of Congress Cataloging-in-Publication Data is available.
  Environment, Climate Change, Endangered Species, Personal Values,
  Family Commitment, Personal Goals
ISBN-13:   978-0-9789753-1-9
ISBN-10:   0-9789753-1-6
Printed in the United States of America
10 9 8 7 6 5 4 3 2 1

To the protectors of the environment,
flora and fauna of our earthly home

1. Solix Assesses the Situation

The arctic summer is coming to an end. It is too soon, for a large number of inhabitants are still trying to store up enough body fat to last through the coming winter. This Arctic summer has been unusual in a number of ways. The spring thaw started much earlier than is normal. The ice pack that covers the Arctic Sea melted faster than usual and to a greater extent. For aeons, the Arctic Sea has been covered with ice, even in mid-June. But this year, by early May, ice packs were already melting and receding at a rapidly accelerating rate. This was only one result of climate changes that residents have seen during this unusual summer. The tundra has supported the weight of caribou for millennia, even in mid-summer. But now, especially in certain parts of the Wasukeki region, even the feet of the fleet-footed grey wolves sink into its slushy, mucky, thawing soil. The surface of the landscape reacts to each step as if it were covered with an enormous carpet made of thick, half-frozen sponges.

Not surprisingly, these unusual conditions have affected the lives of all residents. Birds, Wolves, Caribou, Coyotes, Eagles and even the equally adaptable humans, have struggled to cope with the new environmental reality. In spite of their best efforts, some of the residents have concluded that they must take action to insure their survival, as well as the survival of their entire extended families.

The Inuit have always understood the land and revered the natural forces that govern their homeland. Being among the most adaptable of the human family, they have lived in the Wasukeki region for hundreds of thousands of years. In the process they have acquired a unique understanding, a valuable knowledge base, of the Arctic environment which is their home. Their knowledge is based on natural patterns, with observations passed from generation to generation. As far back in time as anyone can recall, living creatures have relied on natural laws manifested in wind speeds, ice thickness, water currents and other environmental factors.

These natural laws have formed the knowledge base of each species, and particularly of the human inhabitants, whose oral history has communicated this knowledge from generation to generation for aeons, without language- or memory-induced errors.

The recent climate changes, whether natural or originating from more ominous sources, have begun to distort the natural order on which their lives depend. Birds and other animals, though perhaps not as consciously as the Inuit, nonetheless have also noticed the changes. And disrupted weather patterns have influenced the growth cycles of plants. With warmer springs, plants bloom earlier; insects fail to emerge from their winter cover in time to take advantage of the spring bounty of flowers and their sweet energy source, nectar. Consequently, insect populations have declined, due to the smaller food supply. In the fall, a ripple effect will be reflected in the smaller supply of food eaten by voles, birds and other creatures who store up seeds in their winter cache.

One astute observer of these patterns and relationships is a family of birds who in many respects are as wise and adaptable as any living creature, including the hardy Inuit. The extended family of Strix Nebulosa has inhabited the earth since at least the time of the dinosaur, being, in fact, the dinosaur's descendants. Among this family is a branch locally known as the close-knit Nebul family. Nebul family members have benefited from an ingrained education process that passes down certain information so efficiently, and with such a strong impression, that a majority of each individual's adult knowledge base is known at birth. Few other creatures can boast of such an efficient and effective educational process. In less than one–one hundredth of his or her life span, each member of the Nebulosa family possesses ninety percent of all the knowledge he or she will ever acquire. Compared to humans, who require about eighteen percent of their life span to learn the basics, this is astonishing. The Nebul family is even more accomplished. They have become respected by animals and humans alike as wise beyond belief. And even the least learned among the Nebul family achieves this status in record time.

Solix S. Nebul is a young fledgling who will reach maturity within a few months. He has already demonstrated exceptional foresight, benefiting without a single lesson from the effortless passage of certain information between succeeding generations of Nebulosa. Surely there are some things that even members of the Nebul family must learn through example, experience and instruction, but a large portion of their training is passed on during birth. Solix, within a couple of months after hatching, quickly learned additional skills and behaviors from his elders.

He has started to use his knowledge to assess the changing circumstances in the Wasukeki region of the Arctic. He has noticed that his father requires twice as many hunting flights, each twice as long as those of last year, in order to locate the same number of voles. Solix has also noticed, however, that when voles are sighted by his father, they are twice as likely to escape his food-gathering talons. Even so, each vole is more likely to be caught by someone. The net result is that his father has a much harder time feeding his family and himself.

Solix realizes that the earlier springs are part of the problem. Earlier springs, fewer seeds in the fall, and smaller numbers of voles born the following spring, lead to fewer successful hunting trips for his father. Everything in life is connected. Sometimes the effects are immediate; sometimes they are not realized for centuries. Even though Solix has been around for a very short time, he sees evidence of the changing climate.

He knows that vole populations fluctuate over the course of a normal cycle, responding to natural events. His family responds to these variations as well. Three other Nebuls hatched with Solix. The year before, when vole populations were much higher, five fledglings were born to the Nebuls. Solix knows that even with his father's excellent hunting skills, he alone could not have been responsible for the critical decline in vole populations in his territory. As Solix puts it, *"Wo wooho oooow"* meaning "We don't eat *that* much."

Unfortunately, recent events--and accumulated consequences of events past--have affected the whole region. The sweet berries that father Nebul relied on for dessert are now very scarce, because even folk who don't really like them are now eating them.

Polar bears are having a harder time catching their main food, seals. Polar bears have passed on to each succeeding generation their knowledge of the sea ice, its patterns and characteristics. They know that for aeons seals have returned to the Arctic in spring to build dens in snow banks on the sea ice and raise new families. Each seal den has a number of ice holes through which the seals can slip into the sea water to hunt fish or escape a hungry polar bear. The seals typically return in late May, but now the sea ice has begun to melt much earlier than normal. Solix knows that this is not good because it will cause a chain of events that will affect the bears and eventually his own family as well. He thinks, "When a bear catches a seal, there are inevitably scraps of food that are picked up at great risk by ravens, seagulls and other birds who are sometimes on my father's hunting itinerary." Solix concludes, "If bears catch fewer seals, then the birds and other scavengers that my father catches, if any, will not be as fat and tasty."

He sees that the bears are responding to the pressure to find food by increasingly seeking out easier pickings in the village that has grown up near the oil field. They have learned from experience that often there are food scraps at the garbage dump. They also have learned to accept food from strangers who look at them curiously. Solix has often asked his father, "Why do humans put those long shiny objects in front of one eye, and close the other eye, to look at the polar bears?" He has never gotten an answer from his father. But Solix has found that there are certain tricks he can use to get a better fix on the distance to prey. While looking at a potential meal from high above, he has found that when he rotates his head from side to side through a thirty-degree arch while continuously looking at a fixed target, he can more accurately gauge the distance to the target. Even so, he finds it strange that humans carry around those long shiny objects. He feels so lucky that his eyes are perfectly suited to his needs, able even to help him detect temperature variations.

Concerned that the garbage dump is not an ideal dining hall for the polar bears and other animals that have come to depend on it, Solix thinks, "The humans, with the strange shiny objects, are trying to help the polar bears by giving them food that can be found nowhere else in the Wasukeki region. The strange food includes thin things that look like a cross between a flower petal and a pinecone scale. They taste as if they have been soaked in sea water for months, then spread out on a rock to dry for days in the hot summer sun." He adds, "Anyone who eats that strange food will not have to go to the salt lick at the base of Mineral Mountain for months." His father responds, "Yes, they'll get their yearly requirement from just one." Solix laughs, but realizing the effects this could have, he says, "If animals eat the strange food, then the cougars and hawks will get thinner for sure."

Solix and his father see a growing general food crisis in the Wasukeki region. Animals are beginning to panic because they are unable to find sufficient food for themselves and their offspring. Polar bears, which must now cover four times more area in their fruitless, seal-less hunts, are growing weaker even more rapidly than last season. Hunts require a lot of energy, which is usually replaced by the food from successful hunts. Unsuccessful hunts are therefore a double burden.

Solix's own misfortune is becoming evident as well. His father is bringing home less food each day to feed this year's fledglings. His father and mother have to make difficult decisions, given this dwindling food supply; they discuss whether they can continue to raise this year's two surviving fledglings. His father knows it's important to insure that at least one survives, but there is not enough food for both. So he begins to let them determine their own fate by arriving at the nest with food, but rather than putting it directly into a wide-open mouth, he holds it high above the nest so that the fledglings are forced to compete for the few scraps. Over time, the weight difference between the two fledglings increases at an accelerated rate. The stronger, more competitive one grows bigger and bigger, at the expense of the weaker one, but to the benefit of the family as a whole.

Solix learns from this experience that since he is nearing maturity, he must not depend on his father any more. He must rise to his proper place in the family hierarchy and contribute to its success.

Being quite a large bird, Solix often says, "I am the biggest bird in Wasukeki." He needs a dependable supply of food. Voles are his favorite food; he says, "I could eat ten and still have a taste for more." However, Solix also knows that he, too, is spending more time on wing searching for the increasingly elusive creatures. He decides that voles have not become more expert at escaping his sight, but rather there are simply fewer of them to be seen. When Solix questions his father, "How was your hunting today?" he replies, "As lousy as yours!"

"What are we to do?" retorts Solix in an exasperated tone. He quickly injects, "I'll answer that myself. We are big birds, we need an ample supply of voles, and there are not as many as last year, and far fewer than the year before. I must find another food here or another place to hunt voles."

His father looks at him in admiration, seeing that he has used his knowledge base and experience to deduce this important observation. Without uttering a sound, he simply raises a wing as if to say, "Son, you got it and I'm proud of that."

Solix understands and continues, "I'm the biggest bird in these parts, my wing span is now more than five feet, I'm three feet tall, and I need lots of food to keep me going. I need sufficient sustenance to thrive. I need ample food to survive. I'm not going to find the food I need in these parts anymore. Look at me! I'm a beautiful bird and I want to stay that way."

His father agrees, "Yes, I'd hate to see you in a situation like Mr. Polar Bear over there, with skin just hanging over an empty, motionless rib cage!"

2. Food Crisis

At this moment, Solix has a brilliant thought. He decides he will try to deal with the growing local food crisis by setting up a hunting camp at the most distant boundary of his father's territory. That way there will be one less bird around to compete for food.

Then he realizes that this simple approach may not be as straightforward as he originally thought. Remembering, from flying with his father on hunting trips, that the home territory is very irregular in shape, he thinks, "If I am going to the most distant boundary, then I must know where that is. But father's territory is so large that I would be exhausted by measuring the distance to every boundary point." Then, without explanation, he asks his father, "Why didn't you establish a circular territory?"

His father looks very puzzled and replies, "Why do you ask such a thing?"

"Because," Solix responds, "I want to set up a hunting camp at the most distant boundary of your territory, but because the area is so irregular, I don't know where that is. I have only been to the Wasuk River boundary."

"Oh, yes," said his father, "do you remember the distance to Wasuk River?"

"Yes, sir, I do."

"Then it will help you to know that there are only two other places in my territory that are further from here. Each of those places is two minutes' flying time further than Wasuk River, at normal cruising speed. So just fly two minutes further and you'll be on the most distant boundary, or totally outside of my territory. Just be careful there is no headwind during your trip!"

The next morning, at dawn, when the winds are not stirring, Solix takes off toward what he hopes will be an edge of his father's territory. He mentally marks his flight time as he passes over familiar landmarks: Vole Valley– two minutes; toppled pine– three minutes; garbage dump– five minutes. Then suddenly he exclaims, "Oh no, the red Fox and bald Eagle are down there fighting over food again! I think I'll go down and talk to them." He descends gradually so as not to startle either combatant. Upon landing near the ruckus, he inquires, "Why are you fighting over these measly scraps?"

"Because this is all that's available," replies the Fox.

The Eagle interjects, "And I intend to have it all," and at that instant, he tugs with all his strength, pulling the scrap from the Fox, but falling backward. As the Eagle lets out a high-pitched screech, the scrap of food is flung out of his beak. The Fox, being very speedy and a higher jumper, easily springs at least five feet into the air and grabs the food scrap in his mouth like a champion Frisbee dog. The Eagle is very upset with both the Fox and Solix, but by now the Fox is long gone, having devoured his morsel for the day. Solix is just inches from the Eagle, who says, as he scrambles to his feet from his backward tumble, "Well, I guess I'll just have to have *you* for breakfast!"

"Hold on! Not me! " Solix says in a frightened voice. "I may look beautiful but I don't taste good at all!"

At that point the Eagle retorts, "Yes, I know, looks can be deceiving. Because of your butting in, the Fox got away with the food a nice tourist gave me. You probably thought we were fighting over an unclaimed piece of food, when in fact it was mine all along." The Eagle continues his menacing stare at Solix. He then flaps his wings, lifting himself far enough off the ground to place his talons near Solix's neck. Horrified, Solix immediately spins into a defensive posture, his head buried under the canopy of his wings and his tail in the Eagle's face. Settling back to the ground after hovering a few seconds, the Eagle can't contain his laughter, exclaiming "*Eeek, Eeeeek, EeeeeeeK*," for an Eagle, the equivalent of a human belly laugh.

But Solix is not amused. "Why, that's not at all funny," he says indignantly. "You almost got a kung fu talon stab in the stomach."

He then demonstrates, in mock moves meant to intimidate as only a comedian could. Of course nobody, but nobody, in the bird world should try

to frighten a full-grown Eagle, even in jest.   "Umm," the Eagle says with the authority of a commander, "It's clear to me that you are neither a good meal nor a good fighter."

"Well," says Solix, "I'll accept that. Tell you what, since you're in such a good mood, why don't you join me on the trip I'm taking?"

"What trip are you talking about?" says the Eagle.

"I'm on my way to the most distant boundary of my father's territory to set up a new hunting camp. Please join me for an exciting journey.

"May I introduce myself? I am Solix S. Nebul, next to youngest of my father's sons, heir apparent of the Nebulosa clan."

"Pleased to meet you," says the Eagle. "I am Acaetus Hali Leucoc, dominant male of the latest generation of the Leucoc clan, equaled in the bird kingdom only by your extended family, the Nebulosa, and respected by bird, beast and human alike."

At that moment Solix stands at attention as though summoned before a true commandant. He doesn't know what to make of the imposing presence of his new acquaintance. Impressed by his obvious strength and confidence, Solix thinks that this Eagle could make a great hunting partner.

So he says in a humble voice, "Will you join me on the trip? The food will be much better where I'm going."

Knowing that he needs to find a new territory himself, but without confessing that his elders have told him to leave within a month, Acaetus accepts: "Just call me Ace," and he extends his wings to hug Solix.

Just then, a man approaches with a rifle pointed in their direction. Terrified, Solix and Ace dare not make better targets of themselves by taking flight. However, standing still will not protect them, either.   Just as they fear they are doomed, upon hearing the man fire his rifle, they also hear the anguished scream of a polar bear behind them.   The bear that Solix saw at the dump the day before has been seriously wounded. She struggles in a valiant attempt to escape and save her cubs. Unable to lift herself out of the mucky slush at the edge of the dump, she lets out an ear-splitting, window-shattering scream that results, not in pity from the man, but in more gunfire.

The man has been joined by two others with rifles, all intent on killing a polar bear as they laugh in amusement at her plight.

Fortunately for the bear, by this time Solix and Ace have sprung into action. They both know that the she meant no harm to anyone, least of all the humans. She was only trying to find food for herself and thereby provide breast milk for her cubs. Now the two birds fear that three polar bears will be killed by the malice toward one hungry bear. While the men fire over their heads, Solix and Ace hop over toward a ditch providing drainage from the garbage dump. Out of the line of sight of the rifles, Solix and Ace simultaneously lift onto their wings, aided by a strong wind blowing through the ditch as if in a wind tunnel. Instantly both are flying at full speed and pop up out of the ditch like stinger missiles. Powering upward at more than ten feet per second, they are now behind and above the men, whose attention is entirely focused on the struggling polar bear. With their mighty screeches, which frequently curdle the blood of their prey, they startle the men. Together, Solix and Ace are a formidable force to reckon with. By the time the three men regain their composure and turn in the direction of the screeches, they find themselves staring at sixteen razor sharp talons heading directly toward their eyes. Solix and Ace have already coordinated their rescue attack: the man on the right will get three of Solix's talons in his right eye, the one on the left will get three of Ace's talons in his left eye, and the man in the middle will be totally blinded - unless the men retreat quickly, which they do, starting with dives into the muck, followed by hasty, muddy-faced crawling towards the safe space under their truck a few yards away.

Knocking off their hats, Solix and Ace pull out of their threatening dives, and then fly over the abandoned rifles toward the limping polar bear, now safe because she has rolled down a slope into the other end of the ditch, which leads to a large covered culvert under the road. Solix and Ace are relieved to see that she has suffered only a flesh wound. But they also know that the men will not give up so easily. Bent on destroying the polar bear, the men emerge from under the truck, cursing like the sailors they once were. As Solix looks back in their direction, one man runs for the rifles, while another jumps into the driver's seat.   He yells as slivers of glass penetrate his hand that was placed on the seat.

Just then, Solix sees a bunch of keys lying in the mud. With a hairpin turn into a steep dive, he risks his life to snatch the keys before either man is able to react other than by another chorus of swearing. Solix drops the keys into the Nesaku River just a few hundred yards past the culvert. By now, he and Ace have regrouped and begin flying off toward their original destination. Below, they see the polar bear with her two cubs heading into a nearby ice cave. Each glancing at the other, the two birds acknowledge each other's heroism and courage. They now share a strong bond, heightened mutual respect, and the foundation of a lasting friendship.

"Solix, why do you think this happened?"

"Well, spring came very early this year," says Solix, "so by the time the seals arrived, the sea ice had already begun to melt, making it very difficult for the polar bears to eat their usual food. Everybody's got to eat, so I'm sure the bear came to the village dump to find food. That's why we've got to go find new hunting grounds far away from the villages."

As they fly southeast, Ace suddenly spots an unusual sight, a salmon lying on top of the snow. "This is just too much to resist, my favorite food, just lying there for me," he laughs. Without any hesitation, he power-dives toward his hoped-for dinner.

Solix immediately follows because he knows this is not a natural sight: there is no river or stream for miles. Perhaps he could explain a maimed fish lying on the snow after being carried for a long distance and being dropped by someone who had eaten enough. But a perfect, whole salmon in the middle of nowhere, lying on the snow, is just too suspicious!

By now Ace is within a few feet of the salmon. Solix puts on his after-burners–such as he has–and catches up with his friend only inches above the salmon, whereupon he bumps Ace off course, just in time to push him into the snow several inches away from the salmon. Now Ace is fighting mad, not realizing what Solix learned from a prior harrowing experience.

Without a word, Solix picks up a stone with his beak and drops it on the salmon. Crashing out of the snow, just brushing by Ace, the giant black steel jaws of a bear trap cut the up-ended salmon in half. With a sigh of relief, Solix calmly uses his talons to pick up one half of the fish containing roe and foots it to the still shaken Ace.

As they both enjoy the salmon, Solix tells Ace about the large number of animals he has seen caught in such traps, including one of his cousins.

"Solix, this is not the best conversation to have over such a fine dinner!"

"I agree that this was a good dinner, but not fine, in my view. A fine dinner for me would be a few nice plump voles."

"I noticed, Solix, that you finished your half without so much as a pause to savor the flavor."

"Yes, that's because I savor the flavor of voles."

"But you must at least appreciate the value of such a rich source of energy?"

"Oh, sure I do, but voles are a staple of my family's diet and they are becoming rare. I miss being able to go out on a hunt and catch dozens of them to fill my belly."

"Don't you see? That's another advantage of eating salmon. You'd have to catch dozens of voles to fill up, but you need only half a salmon."

"Good point, 'cause I *am* stuffed!" says Solix. "But on the other wing, a dozen voles would be fifty times more satisfying to me than half a salmon."

Then Solix thinks, "Maybe I'd better start adjusting my diet and develop a taste for other foods. It seems vole populations are declining everywhere." He has flown for a full day across the vast expanse of his father's territory, and he hasn't seen a single vole. Disappointment sets in at the prospect that even at the territorial boundary, there may be no more voles. On that note, he dozes off for the night.

Seeing Solix asleep, Ace thinks it's been a successful day in spite of the difficulties they've encountered. Ace and his family have overcome hardships before. Once having been on the brink of extinction, they all have a fuller appreciation of life. Soon he, too, drifts into a deep sleep, eager to see the next sunrise.

3. Conflicts Flare Up

Ace dreams about the fight he had with the red Fox over a small piece of food that was not nearly as succulent as tonight's fine salmon. He dreams about the confrontation with the three men and worries that they may retaliate. They are surely marooned at the native village, far from their duty stations at the new drilling platform he flew over yesterday. There is no way they will ever get the truck keys out of the river. Hopefully, he thinks, one of them will have another set of keys so they can just leave. All night long, his sleep is interrupted by nightmares about the tensions in the Wasukeki region.

As dawn breaks, Solix awakens to a beautiful sunrise, but he is still sleepy. With the short summer nights his usual night hunting routine is modified anyway, so he appreciates yesterday's salmon dinner more than usual. He also realizes that he and Ace can't fly all day again today. He usually sleeps during the day, though Ace usually sleeps at night. For that reason, he thinks they are an odd pair. On the other wing, he thinks it would be a tremendous advantage to both of them if they could work together. With different hunting targets, different tastes, and different sleep patterns, they could both benefit from their differences. Solix shouts, "Ace, wake up! How would you like to be my partner? We could join forces and increase our chances of survival. You know my family is threatened with extinction. I am a rare bird, you know."

"Yes, I do know," says Ace. "My family and I have had a lot of experience with the challenges of re-building after being on the brink."

These words are an understatement, revealing only superficially the wounds from the nearly mortal blows dealt to Ace's extended family. After many, many years of effort, they are just beginning to re-establish themselves in home territories that previously had been theirs for aeons. Ace's family had been poisoned by treated water sprayed by the humans on their own crops. And they could never figure out why the humans would

27

poison themselves, even if they didn't care about or realize the impact on Ace's family.

"Well then, we should work together," says Solix.

"I agree," says Ace, still keeping his little secret.

"Hooray!" says Solix. "It's a beautiful day."

"You know, Solix, any day that I am here to witness is a beautiful day!"

At this point, Solix turns slowly toward Ace and says solemnly, "Any day that *we* can see is a beautiful day!" For they are well aware of the fragility of life's balance and of life itself. Slight disruptions of nature's ebb and flow can have unforeseen, disastrous ripple effects.

"Solix, you did a great job arbitrating my dispute with the red Fox."

"Thanks."

It is clear that Solix and Ace have great respect for each other. More and more, they have come to appreciate their differences and recognize the strengths developing in each of them from these differences. Ace sees Solix as a great arbitrator with wisdom beyond his age. And Solix believes Ace exceeds the high expectations that come with being a member of the Leucoc branch of the Leucoce family. No other bird family is as revered. Eagles reign supreme as a symbol of many values for birds as well as humans.

Both Solix and Ace are struggling, trying to lead their families out of a continuing crisis. Climate changes are just the most recent calamities that have beset their families, which six hundred years ago were both doing exceedingly well. However, a long sequence of events during the last four centuries has nearly wiped them off the face of the earth.

As a result, this trip takes on more significance for the two friends than even they realize. Hanging in the balance is not only their own survival, but also the re-growth of their entire species, especially Solix's. As if realizing this, Solix says, "Let's go. The territorial boundary is waiting for us."

On that note, they unfold their wings, lift into the air on a strong breeze, and fly as only they can to reach the next thermal that will help propel them on their still long journey. Within minutes, each is flying at speeds exceeding a hundred miles per hour. Effortlessly soaring above the clouds on fixed, broadly outstretched wings, they soon approach the territorial boundary. "Wasuk River is below!" exclaims Solix.

He then explains to Ace that they are now two minutes' flying time from the most distant boundary. Solix calculates the point on the ground which they will be directly above after another two minutes' level flight. He then picks a landmark rock outcropping to navigate toward. On his signal, both flex muscles in their left wings to create more wing curvature and thus more lift on that side, then gently turn right as their right wings dip toward the ground far below. They have entered a gentle, thirty-degree, counter-clockwise controlled spiral that periodically takes them directly over their chosen rock outcropping as they descend. It's beautiful evidence of the perfection of their aerodynamic design. Within ten minutes, they arrive at the chosen landmark on the ground without making a single adjustment in their flight path. It's confirmation of Solix's ability to navigate with great precision.

As they descended, Solix had also been scanning the landscape for voles. He saw none. Meanwhile, Ace had focused on the Wasuk River as they periodically passed over it.

4. The Decision to Move

The two feathered friends land on a staircase of ledges that overlook the Wasuk River in the distance. This is a pristine wilderness area. As they look toward the west they get a view of the old growth forest that extends from the banks of the river to as far as the eye can see. At the top of the rock ledges on which they now sit, the forest continues to blanket the landscape, also extending eastward beyond the horizon. The forest contains an amazing array of plants and animals. Douglas Firs and Ponderosa Pines are the giants of this part of the forest, with, interspersed among them, an astonishing variety of other trees--Hemlock, Red Oak, White Oak, Pin Oak, Spruce, and numerous others. Then there are the smaller plant species, such as Dogwood trees, Juniper shrubs and other varieties that are even more numerous than the trees. Completing the lineup of plant life is a mind-boggling array of different bushes, grasses, vines, so many different plants that it has taken humans centuries to discover, list, categorize and describe them. Even now they are still finding new ones.

The level of understanding humans have acquired concerning the role of all these plants in nature's scheme is even more limited than their knowledge of the ecosystem's dependencies. The native peoples of this region know a lot about the plants indigenous to their homelands, having lived off the land in perfect harmony with nature for millions of years. They had learned to live with nature and to benefit from its bounty. Their hunting practices were honed by close observation of their animal neighbors. When hunting, they never take more than needed to provide for themselves and their tribes. They use every part of each animal, first blessing it for sacrificing itself for the benefit of the native tribes, who respect their benefactors by including them in their cultural rituals. Eagles and Owls, along with many other animals, hold a special place in their lives.

Solix explains to Ace, "The Wasuk River itself is a mighty river that flows from and among the mountains."

Starting at a very high elevation, it is little more than a collection of water droplets from the leaves of trees and other plants that have cushioned the falling rain before it hits the earth. Every raindrop cascades down from the sky in a rhythmic journey that takes it from a tree top to more than a hundred bounces off successive leaves, needles and branches, on the way down through the forest canopy. Not a single drop on the forest escapes such a journey. Some journeys are shorter, starting at the tops of shrubs, or even blades of grass, but seen in two dimensions, each path is a zigzag from top to bottom, sky to earth, with each change of direction aided by a leaf or stem along the path. Having reached the earth this way, the water has already performed its initial task in the scheme of nature, bathing each plant in the best way possible. By the time the raindrops reach the ground, their fall through thousands of feet has been cushioned to the point where their impact is no more than pitter-patter on the forest floor. Were it not for the plants, each rain drop would be like a small bomb, accelerating from its formation thousands of feet above, and hitting the ground to create billions of minute craters, and eroding the soil to such an extent that the resulting micro-tributaries would be forty-sixty percent dirt. As it is, however, the water in the micro-tributaries is as clear as the crystal raindrops that fell on the forest canopy.

Zillions of raindrops formed in clouds thousands of feet above the earth and fell onto the forest plants. Countless un-mapped micro-tributaries flow off the plants. Can we really say exactly where Wasuk River starts? Can we really pinpoint the exact place of its birth, other than to say it started far above the clouds? Even at its highest elevation, the river benefits from the many micro-tributaries that converge to form rivulets, then bigger streams, then creeks, all collectively feeding its flow. If the flow is too slow, then the water is a puddle, pond or lake. But once the flow reaches a certain speed, it's a river until it becomes a lake, sea or ocean. If the volume is too small, then it's a micro-tributary, rivulet, creek, or stream.

Solix believes that, "Rivers are best viewed as having many starting points, but only one *source* which isn't even on earth."

Irrespective of where Wasuk River started, it surely must have been a beautiful birth. As it twists and turns to make its way down the mountain passes into the broad, lush valley, its course appears as though laid out by an accomplished landscape architect. The truth is much simpler but more beautiful. The course of each individual drop has been determined, at each and every position, by the elegant interaction of a primary force, gravity. Water drops that have fallen and run across Wasuk plateau during the past billion years carved the river's course. Nothing could be more beautiful than that simple process. Nothing could have produced scenery that is more spectacular.

Directly below the rock ledges, the river makes a sweeping eighty-degree turn from southeast to northwest. As the river makes this turn, it undercuts the rocks at the base of the ledges, creating a pattern that is repeated all the way up to the top of the ridge. It is clear that several geological processes have shaped the exquisitely sculpted rock ledges, with the river acting as a cutting tool to carve a crescent shape into the rock face at the water level. The level of the rock is pushed gradually upward each year as tectonic plates well below the earth's surface push the ledges higher. The earth's crust in this region consists of alternating layers of hard and soft sandstone. The undercuts occur when soft sandstone is exposed to the river current. These factors have produced a colossal natural amphitheater with crescent-shaped steps of equal height and identical cantilevering. The steps themselves are fourteen inches thick, while the undercuts are four inches high. Perhaps most astonishing is the fact that the top surface of each step is perfectly level. Some local natives call these the Stairway of the Gods.

On the opposite bank, a crescent-shaped sandy shore forms a beach worthy of the most beautiful tropical island. The churning of the water creates whitecaps that give a foamy appearance to the surface, except in the middle of the river between the two cusps created by slightly submerged rocks. There the river's surface is exceptionally smooth, mirroring all the light that strikes it. The native peoples call this point of the river Imikenu, meaning "the eye used by the great one to watch over us". Solix calls this

33

point the "Eye of the Hawk" because it reminds him of the piercing gaze of an attacking broadtail hawk.

Solix and Ace are excited by the beauty of this valley and its potential as their new home. However, both know that other details have to be investigated before key decisions are made. As they turn their heads side to side to survey the beautiful scenery one last time, their eyes meet.

"Ace, isn't this a perfect setting?"

"Well, Solix, it certainly is beautiful! But we have a few things to check out before making a final decision."

"Of course, I've got to find some voles, and you've got to locate some fish!"

"Ok, so let's get to work," says Ace.

At that moment, both birds launch themselves into the wind sweeping up from the rock ledges. It's a perfect ascent powered by the high altitude winds that are funneled by the mountains into the narrow pass further downriver from Imikenu. Solix soars skyward and heads south to survey the high plateau. Ace first ascends, then smoothly glides westward and down toward the sand bar at the edge of Imikenu. What they see includes a lot more than voles and fish. More rabbits than voles. More minnows and trout than salmon. More trees than meadows. More pines than Hemlocks.

Ace is anxious as he approaches the river, hopeful that he will find a bounty of fat salmon. After several low passes up and down the river, above and below Imikenu, Ace realizes that there are no salmon here. Undeterred, he looks for other sources of sustenance. What he sees on closer inspection is promising. Smaller fish are numerous in certain parts of the river. They are all smaller than his favorite salmon, many much smaller, but he judges a few to be almost the size of a small river-bound salmon. "Whoa!" he yells out, "I've found the golden roe." He knows it's not really golden roe, his most prized gourmet food, but something just as good.

As he listens to the echo of his voice he hears a faint, unrecognized sound. He has yelled so loudly that even his echo is much louder than the unfamiliar sound that he strains to hear. At least detecting the direction from which it is coming, he swirls in mid-air to follow the new sound toward its source.

After a few more flaps of his wings, Ace sees the most beautiful young Eagle he has ever had the pleasure of meeting. Sitting on a branch near the top of the tallest ponderosa pine in sight, she perks up when she sees Ace come into view. They both cry out so loudly it disturbs every creature within earshot. Ace asks, "What is your name? Do you live here?" Before her response, the two of them are soaring above the forest in happy flights. She appears as happy to see him as he is to see her. But Ace can't imagine anyone being happier than he. He flirts, "You are so happy that it's infectious!" Still he gets no verbal response; only her body language signals joy. Now he is panting as he attempts to keep up with her speedy retreat.

This leads him out over the low shrubs and birch that line parts of the westerly riverbank, higher over the junipers further from shore. He is now high enough to see the western forest for miles. He keeps his ears tuned. It's a new voice, an Eagle's voice, responding to his yells. Now he can hear words, "You must be new around here! Because all of us local Eagles know there are lots of fish along this stretch of Wasuk River." Now Ace is worried: has he offended someone whom he might have befriended?

At that moment, he decides, "Nobody, but nobody, out flies me!" He increases his wing beats to sixty per minute. Then ninety per minute. Then in a flash he careens by the pursued, as if shot from a cannon. Now he really has a problem, how to slow down before she thinks he is racing her. That would be ungentlemanly, so he puts on the brakes, lowering his feet and bringing his wings to near vertical even though he is in level flight. That does the trick: now he is right alongside her. He thinks, "It's definitely a lady! How lucky can I be?" He says, "Hi, my name is Ace. I'm new here!" No verbal response, but an arched eyebrow and a sweet smile are his reward.

Now he is beside himself, Ace thinks, "Plenty of fish, plenty of trees in which to build a nest, and plenty of room to fly! And to top it off, I've

found a very beautiful--" Before he can complete that thought, she has flown off again in a different direction.

Now he thinks, "She's shy, pretty and fast too!" In those few seconds, she is now hundreds of feet above him. He takes a couple of deep breaths and then launches himself into an almost vertical climb. Now they both dart about the sky, upward faster than ever imagined. Hovering as though they were humming birds. Diving as though falcons. Circling like tornados. Creating a spectacle! If birds have the capacity to love, then this is certainly love at first flight! Ace continues chasing the alluring but evasive partner.

He wonders, "Is she trying to escape or leading me on a wild Eagle chase?" Just then he receives a partial answer. She brushes by him at a speed exceeding that of a boulder falling from fifty feet above, the origin of her latest sortie. Their right and left wings touch ever so slightly along the front edges of their primary feathers. They then spin in a circle, as though hanging onto the spindle of a merry-go-round.

Everything that has happened since he first set eyes on her is new to him. Winded and windblown, he is determined to keep pace with the natural-born flyer who is now showing him new maneuvers on each pass. He mimics every mid-air move she displays. Soon it seems as simple as the rules that govern the flow of water to the sea. The resulting mid-air flourishes are also beautiful. They have floated effortlessly to hundreds of feet above the forest canopy. Circling, stalling in mid-air, diving, tumbling, it's an aerial acrobatics exhibition. And then, as though they have used all their energy and lost their ability to breathe or fly, they fall toward each other, at an unthinkable speed, to grab each other talon to talon, as their wings arch backward in a purposeful V. Now they are falling like bricks, faster and faster toward the ground, as their feathers flutter in the turbulent air. Increasingly, their wings are buffeted by the apparent wind created by their speedy fall. Clockwise circles, upside-down tumbles, counter-clockwise helixes, in a matter of minutes they display a seemingly endless repertoire of aerobatic stunts.

At the last second before crashing into the tallest ponderosa, they release talons, re-configure their wings and pull out of the free fall, to fly back to a high altitude and repeat the ritual all over again--and again. While anyone should expect such a spectacular display to attract attention, in this case, it comes from an unwelcome source. In the far distance, another Eagle squawks, with the authority of age and the dominance of the pecking order. His sounds are familiar to Ace but as unwelcome as a broken wing. Ending the last talon-joined free fall, Ace and his hoped–for mate fly toward the tall ponderosa where he had first seen her.

Out of nowhere, from the opposite direction comes the biggest Eagle that Ace has ever seen. He is the ruler of these parts, the dominant male of this territory, which Ace thought he could claim as his own. Unfortunately, Ace's new friend is clearly known by the approaching eagle, perhaps she is a member of his extended family. Is she his daughter, granddaughter, niece, cousin or mate for life? At this moment Ace has no way of knowing. However, he knows that in any case, he has broken a sacred rule of the Leucoce family.

As soon as he sees the dominant male and hears his further loud protests, he knows that if he does not leave immediately, love or life, but not both, will be his destiny in the Wasuk River valley. Though he is exhausted, and heart- broken, his wings flap harder and faster than ever before, almost endangering his heart. Out of breath and greatly disappointed, Ace arrives back at his perch.

It is not long before Solix returns too. Standing at attention, Ace demands a report from Solix, "All present and accounted for?"

"Aye, aye, Sir," he hears in response.

"Your report?"

Solix continues more loudly, "I found only a few voles! I would consume them in a week!"

Then Ace retorts, "We certainly can't stay here, can we?"

"No, sir!" barks Solix.

Whereupon Ace concludes they must come up with a plan to move further south. Solix's protest is halfhearted because, for different reasons, he has come to the same conclusion. Now Ace has two secrets, and the last one he considers especially private. Without asking Ace for a report, Solix confides, "We've had no luck here, have we?"

Turning toward the distant ponderosa far below, Ace says, "We must call for a Council of the Elders right away. We must inform them of our decision to venture further south to find suitable new home territories. We must get their blessings."

Solix voices agreement. Ace salutes and Solix hops to attention and salutes in one continuous motion.

"You stay here. I will go call for a Council with the Elders," says Ace as he flies off in a rush. As soon as he crosses Wasuk River, he again hears warnings from the biggest Eagle he has ever seen. He cautiously approaches the area from which the warnings are radiating. Solix hears the commotion and wonders if he should continue to follow orders. But suddenly, everything is quiet. Below, Ace puts on a display of contrition, apology and humility as he slowly approaches the tree where he saw perched the biggest Eagle he's ever seen. With head lowered, he lands on a limb five feet below the limb occupied by the dominant Eagle. He continues to hold his head well below horizontal. In silence, he waits nervously for a response, hoping his apology has been accepted, but on guard for a punishing attack.

"Are you lost?" Before Ace can mumble an answer, he hears, "Did the high winds blow you off course?"

Ace swallows, clears his gullet and begins an almost silent reply but is again interrupted, "Do you have a reasonable explanation for being in Wasuk River Valley?"

"Sir, I have come to request that you convene a meeting of the Council of Elders," Ace says with humility that hides his confidence. "I am seeking to establish a new territory, outside the range of any already claimed land. I am the son of Acaetus Hail Leucoc of the northern Wasukeki region. I have embarked on a journey to discover new territory that I may claim without dispute. Clearly this area is not what I'm looking for."

Admiring that Ace has understood his protests, without uttering a sound, the dominant male moves threateningly on his perch. Ace hears the flutter of wings, but dares not look up for fear of being dispatched by razor-sharp talons. He listens intently, without raising so much as an eyelid, trying to figure out what is happening. There's more commotion from above. Shaking inside, struggling to suppress his muscle tremors, but maintaining his outward composure, Ace continues to listen from the posture of a submissive subject.

Then he hears the most beautiful voice he has ever heard. He thinks, "Could this be her?"

"Father," she says, "I met this gentleman after hearing him celebrating his discovery of the bounty of Wasuk River."

"What is his name?" asks a deep authoritative voice, which Ace knows is that of the biggest Eagle.

"I don't know," says the sweet voice.

"Then you didn't meet him properly," replies the melodic baritone.

"May I ask your name?" she says shyly.

Hesitating for a moment, Ace says, "I am Acaetus Hali Leucoc, of the latest generation of the Leucoc clan of the northern Wasukeki region."

The most beautiful voice then says, "I am Halia Hali Leucoce, and this is my father, King Accip Hali Leucoce."

Continuing his submissive display, Ace slowly spreads his wings, arching them backwards, and extending them fully, below and behind the limb on which he is perched. "Pleased to meet you, Sir I chanced upon your daughter during my survey of this boundary of the Wasukeki region. I apologize for any inconvenience I may have caused you." He continues, "I request that you call a meeting of the Council of Elders so that I may--" He is interrupted by the loud clearing of King Accip's throat.

Pausing for several seconds, a seeming eternity to both him and Halia, Ace continues, "I request that you call a meeting of the Council of Elders so that I may ask for approval to establish a new territory much further south of Wasuk River."

"Well, then," announces King Accip, "it appears that you have good intentions, so I will send out the call." By now Halia is straining to contain her excitement and just barely succeeds, as she thinks about the next questions she is hopeful Ace will ask.

"You are dismissed," King Accip declares.

Ace is finally able to resume his stature with dignity, for in the subtle tones of Accip's voice he hears both acceptance and acknowledgement of his atonement. He gathers his wings as his legs push forward into a slow, graceful exit, gliding toward the ground and then circling in a broad turn toward Wasuk River and the ledges beyond. Halia sees that he is heading toward what they call Kolob Ridge, one the grandest natural amphitheaters in the Wasukeki Region.

As Ace flies back to tell Solix the plan, he hears the Council calls echoing through the Valley. Solix hears them as well but doesn't understand what they mean. Soon, Ace is again standing next to his friend. Ace listens as the echoes of the Council calls reverberate through the Valley. He now knows that Solix's presence has also been detected by King Accip because the Council call instructs all elders of the Leucoce and Nebulosa families to gather for a Grand Council. Unbeknownst to Ace and Solix, the rock ledge on which they perch is the only site in the region used for such Grand Council sessions.

Within minutes, dozens of birds arrive at Kolob Ridge. "What's going on, Ace?" Solix asks.

"I requested a Council of the Leucoce Elders, but a summons has been issued to both our families. It appears that the Council will convene right here."

Just then, one of the recent arrivals asks Ace, "What tribe do you represent?"

"Oh, I don't represent any tribe at this point, but I hope to soon." With that utterance, the locals know that these are the birds to be judged. The two friends are summarily advised that these are the Kolob Ridge Council Chambers. As they are ushered off to their proper place at the bottom of Kolob Ridge, on the shore of Kolob Creek, Ace and Solix discuss their prospects.

"What happened over there, Ace? Who did you talk to? Why are all these birds flying onto this ridge?" asks Solix as he nearly panics. By now the sky is filled with so many wings that they cast as many shadows as the passing clouds.

Before Ace can answer, the steps of Kolob Ridge are filled with hundreds of family members. The fly-in continues through the night, with arrivals from the Nebulosa family. And the following morning, members of the Leucoce family continue to arrive. Soon the steps on the right side of Kolob Creek are filled by Leucoce. The Nebulosa are perched on the left side of the creek. All are perched in the proper pecking order.

Just then King Accip alights on top of a rock archway over Kolob Creek. To his right, an assistant picks up a chicken-egg-sized pebble and begins flying toward Wasuk River. As the assistant reaches altitude and speed, he drops the rock, hitting a precise location on Kolob Ridge. Upon impact, the pebble plays an arpeggio of musical notes as it bounces down the steps before finally shattering and falling into the Wasuk River with a cymbalistic splash. Ace and Solix look at each other as they think, "What beautiful music!" So occupied are they by the music calling the session to order that they fail to hear King Accip's initial words.

"What did he say, Ace?" Solix waits for an answer as the assistant lands next to them and proceeds to usher them down to a log over Kolob Creek.

Ace is somewhat apprehensive. Solix notices and is even more nervous because he knows less about what's happening than Ace. He also sees Ace staring at an isolated figure peering from behind a giant Hemlock, but he can't figure out who it is. Ace keeps staring and begins to smile. Solix repeatedly tries to see who it is. Just then a peek from behind the Hemlock reveals that a beautiful Leucoc or Leucoce maiden is ogling Ace. When Ace starts to ogle back, Solix give him a swift, hard, almost unnoticed, wing to the stomach. "She's just wishing us good luck," Ace whispers in a muted but excited voice. "They're asking us to make our case for moving further south to set up new territories."

"Why didn't you tell me this before? I'm a nervous wreck here! You want me to have a heart attack?" Solix questions Ace in rapid succession.

"No, I want you to make your case as convincingly as possible to the Nebulosa families. I will make my case to the Leucoce families. They will each then caucus and send a delegate to sit with King Accip on the Supreme Council."

"I haven't had time to prepare a case. Have you, Ace? Is that why your scouting trip took so much longer than mine? Is that why that Leucoce maiden is responding to your ogling? I need some answers here and now!" demands Solix.

Just then the Council assistant commands the intruders to be silent and directs each toward his respective family. As they part, Solix looks anxiously at Ace, thinking it may not be a good thing that Ace is being moved closer to the peeking Maiden. But now each is positioned at the center of the bottom ledge in front of their respective families. Neither can hear the other as the Council elders begin questioning each of them.

"Solix, what have you gotten yourself into? Why was it necessary for King Accip to summon us here?--" Solix interrupts, "I think I can explain everything that I know..." as he thinks "...and some things that I can only guess about."

"Well then, let's hear your case!" says an impatient elder.

Thinking quickly on his feet, Solix begins, "To all the elders here assembled, and in the name of my forefathers, and for the benefit of future generations of the Nebulosa family, I humbly submit my request to leave Wasukeki Region in order to establish my own territory further south. I make this request because, after being granted permission by my father to explore the most distant boundary of his territory, I have found this area unsuitable. There are not enough voles in these parts for my taste, nor sufficient numbers to support the family that I hope to raise. I need to move further south in my effort to find a suitable territory. My case is made more complicated by the partnership that I have struck with Mr. Acaetus Hali Leucoc over there. It's a long story, but he has become a very good friend and ally. We both want to establish new territories together because both of our families will benefit from such an arrangement. I respectfully request your approval to move further south. We're young adults just coming into our prime. We now know we need to establish our own territory somewhere. Everyone will benefit from your approval."

Meanwhile, Ace is also responding to his inquisition with style, though his position is direr. When asked to explain his actions, he begins just as Solix did, with a dignified and well-thought-out, though hastily assembled, petition. But before he can get past the third word, a Leucoce elder interrupts, "What possessed you to trespass on Wasuk Territory?"

"I can explain."

"Who granted you the right to embrace Halia?"

Now Ace gets really worried because for the first time he realizes that the territorial matter, which he thought was settled, may not be the only issue confronting him. At this thought he becomes visibly nervous: his legs tremble. He knows the fate of anyone who is judged to have broken the rule referenced by the last question.

"Sir," he says politely, "please allow me to explain everything."

"If you can. We will listen."

"I came here after failing to find sufficient food in northern Wasukeki Region. I got into a fight with a red Fox, and Solix over there intervened. We subsequently became friends and agreed to partner to find a new territory that we could establish. Since Solix had the permission of his elders to explore this area, we arrived here with the intent of establishing a new territory. Of course, that meant that we were not intending to stake a claim on any territory already ruled by someone else in either family. After a scouting trip, Solix determined that this area was unsuitable for him because there are not enough voles. We have decided to move further south. I respectfully request your permission to establish a new territory further south." Ace declares, having anticipated further questioning "I am only requesting that you allow me to join Solix in establishing a new territory."

Hearing this from behind the Hemlock, Halia is disappointed but hopeful that Ace will ask about her later in the session. Ace continues to make his case, "The Wasukeki Region is experiencing a food crisis resulting in part from climate changes and in part from natural fluctuations in vole populations. Salmon are not as plentiful, either. My fight with a red Fox occurred when I was in a village accepting food from a tourist. But the Fox was hungry too and took my food."

"You let a red Fox take your food? Are you worthy of a new territory? Are you worthy of leading a new branch of the family?" shouts a Leucoc elder.

"Sir, with all due respect, I submit that I am. You see, I didn't let the Fox have the food. It happened while three men were shooting at us!"

At this pronouncement, every Leucoce and Leucoc is horrified that their treaty with the humans has been broken. They begin asking for details. Ace realizes that he has unintentionally raised an even bigger issue before the Council. Their concern is so great that they end their questioning on territorial matters and focus instead on the broken truce. Ace is relieved but also worries that he may have opened a Pandora's Box.

Almost simultaneously, the two young friends are dismissed by the Councils. Halia is disappointed.

The two newly elected officials of the Supreme Council approach the top of Kolob Ridge. As they seat themselves, each on the side of the creek above his family, King Accip (who will continue to reign at their pleasure for another two years) acknowledges their presence. "What are your recommendations to the Supreme Council?" he asks.

The Leucoc member strongly recommends that the Supreme Council declare sanctions against the humans. Both Accip and the Nebulosa member are astonished. There is general confusion in the Supreme Council.

"Hold on here, this is not on the agenda for this Council meeting!" Accip addresses the other Supreme Council members. Fortunately, none of the other assembled delegates can hear the discussion in the Supreme Council. When the matter is finally presented to the larger Council, endless debate

ensues. Of course, they too were taken aback by the turn of events, and the debates exhaust everyone including Halia. She was fatigued by straining to listen to the council proceedings and by her fear of being detected and punished.

Finally, the Council assistant, on King Accip's orders, calls the full Council of Elders as well as the Supreme Council to order. King Accip stands again on the stone arch and announces, "The request, from Acaetus Leucoc and Solix Nebul, to work together to establish new territories further south is hereby granted. All other matters before this Council of Elders are hereby tabled for later consideration."

With that, Ace and Solix flutter their wings in celebration as they march out of the Council chamber.

The proceedings have ended none too soon, because the sun is setting at Kolob Ridge, leaving only the night lights of the Aurora Borealis. As these appear, Ace and Solix, with the blessings of their families, hasten their plans to leave. In the rush, Halia has hastened away, first by hopping further into the shrubs near the Hemlock, then flying low, skimming up over Wasuk River toward a small clearing where she turns sharply to the left, ascending toward the tallest ponderosa pine. All the while, she prays that no one has seen her.

While others take off for the roosts assigned by King Accip, Ace and Solix sit down to plan their epic journey. They agree to embark the following morning. The increasingly intense night lights to the north indicate to them that winter snows will be heavier soon. Even now, a light blanket of snow covers parts of the high plateau above Kolob Ridge.

Solix has settled down for the short night. But Ace is still awake: he can't sleep, wondering what happened to Halia and how he will ever get approval from King Accip. He lurches off his perch several times as he dreams about meeting Halia. Solix awakens at dawn, eager to leave.

5. The Epic Journey Begins

His friend's youthful enthusiasm should stir Ace, but it doesn't. Eager to embark on their epic journey, Solix laments Ace's slow response, "Come on, bird, let's get moving." After much prodding and poking, he is finally able to get Ace to open one eyelid, then a second, and then a third. He figures that Ace is now at least half-awake, maybe even three-quarters. Ace struggles to remove the cobwebs from his eyes. Since he did not sleep well, he is sluggish and drowsy.

"Ace, there were more snow flurries last night. We need to get going before the snow gets heavier."

To this Ace slurs a half-asleep response, "I heard you, I heard you, leave me alone."

"No!" shouts Solix, approaching Ace in a menacing way. "We have a duty to get going and establish our new territories further south. The Council is depending on us. Now that they have approved our request, we are obligated to carry it out. And if we don't, we will be disgraced."

This last word arouses Ace. He is thinking, "If I am disgraced, then I will never have a chance to complete the falling talon ritual with Halia."

"Okay, okay, hold your birds! I'm fully awake now!" he says, thinking, "But if I leave without seeing Halia, how will she know that I plan to return for her? How will she know my intentions?" At this point he says, "I can't leave just yet! I have some business to take care of."

"Yes, Ace, I know what your business is. You want to go off to see that Leucoce maiden that I saw yesterday behind the Hemlock," says Solix.

"Well, you're right; I do want to let her know that I plan to return for her."

"But don't you see, that's a very risky proposition for you, for us! You don't know her. She is clearly a member of the Leucoce, and not the Leucoc, family. Have you gotten permission to talk to her from the Leucoce elders?"

"I have met her as well as her father," Ace says proudly.

"When did you do that, during the Council meeting yesterday?" scowls Solix.

"Well no, not at the Council."

"Now the truth comes out: you met them when you were supposed to be scouting the area west of the Wasuk River."

Ace then admits his error and apologizes while trying to get Solix to understand: "I have never seen anyone more beautiful. Her name is Halia, isn't that a beautiful name? It was love at first sight. I'm deeply in love. Her father is Accip."

"HER FATHER IS KING ACCIP? Well, if you don't come to your senses right away, you'll be deadly in love!" exclaims Solix. Then, in a mellower tone, he asks "Did you talk to her? Does she know your feelings? She knows that we are leaving to establish a new territory further south because she was there listening to the Council proceedings the whole time. I think what you should do is come with me now and come back for her later. If it really was love at first sight, she also knows how you feel and will wait for you to return."

For Ace these are comforting words. Hearing this wisdom from Solix, he is more prepared to undertake the epic journey. "Just give me a couple of minutes to gather my thoughts, please."

"Okay, Ace, I understand your dilemma. Take a few minutes to think about it. I want you to be sure of your decision; because once we leave, there will be no turning back."

"Right." says Ace as he ponders his choices. Then he says to Solix, "I already made a bargain with you to join you in settling a new southern territory. I will keep my promise. I will leave with you at sunrise."

Solix is relieved and pleased, but sees the sadness in Ace's eyes. He knows that he is making a huge personal sacrifice. "I appreciate what you're doing, Ace. I know it was a tough decision for you, but I think you made the right choice." Just then Solix thinks, "It would not be against protocol for me to pay a quick visit to Halia." With that thought, he slips away quietly as though to give Ace a bit of privacy. Ace is so deep in thought about Halia that he doesn't notice the departure.

Solix's stealth pays off mightily in this situation. Following the river downstream, he flies off without even a whisper, minimizing the chance that Ace will see him leaving. In a few seconds, his swift wings propel him between the trees as he weaves his way through the west bank forest. He stops only once to inquire where he may find King Accip, believing that Halia will likely be nearby. He figures that this question will raise few suspicions. A local resident points the way and Solix continues his mission. Soon, he emerges into a small clearing in the forest. Straight ahead, he again sees the beautiful Leucoce maiden. As he approaches her, she is brimming with excitement. "Quiet," says Solix as he whispers something to her. She smiles, he leaves. It is a split-second encounter, just long enough to convey a critical message. Before Halia has a chance to say anything, she sees Solix flying off toward the river.

By the time Solix quietly alights and hops up to where Ace is still deep in thought, the sun is breaking over Kolob Ridge. "Okay, Ace, all preparations have been made for our departure. Let's go!"

Ace turns to him and says, "We'll take the familiar Pacific route that the elders have suggested."

"Aye, aye, Commander!" says Solix with a broad smile as they both lift off from the ridge. As they fly, the treetops and then the whole valley erupts in joyful squawks and screeches, hoots and howls. The elders are giving them a grand send-off. In spite of the loud songs, Ace hears only one voice, a beautiful, distinctive melody from the one he cherishes. He looks back in the direction of the tallest ponderosa pine. Solix sees this and immediately knows why. "Ace, I believe everything will be fine. We need to focus on the task at wing." With that Ace turns his head to the southerly direction in which they are flying.

After several hours of catching thermals to soar and glide high above, Ace and Solix have covered a lot of ground. Even though they have used a modest amount of energy to travel this great distance, they are beginning to feel hunger pangs. "Solix, it's time for us to make a re-fueling stop, don't you agree?"

"Yes, Commander, that will be necessary."

"Then we'll glide to a lower altitude to begin scanning the landscape. Solix, you go down to one hundred feet and I'll stay at five hundred."

Solix agrees this will be a good strategy for quickly scanning a broad area. Ace will look for distant indicators of the best re-fueling spot and direct Solix in for a closer inspection. He knows that Solix is the stealthiest flyer in the sky. His noiseless flight will enable Solix to more easily conduct his reconnaissance without causing any stir.

Within minutes, Ace dips his right wing to signal that Solix should take a closer look to the right of their flight path. Solix banks and swoops down even closer to the ground. In seconds he has covered several hundred yards as he quietly power-dives toward the series of hills that run parallel to their course. Because he is at a lower altitude, he has not seen the small river just beyond one of the hills. But as he continues to fly in that direction, he hears the sound of a waterfall, the sound of a white-water river. Within a few seconds, Solix sees it, running alongside a sheer cliff, which he estimates is three hundred yards dead ahead. He looks up, and at this point, Ace is maintaining his altitude, straight above him. Solix swoops down for an even closer look.

Without a sound he sends out the "fish below" signal to Ace, who, without further ado, streaks down to the white-water river. In the blink of an eye, he sights and targets a fish in the river. His aim is precise and deadly. His talons make a splash as they spear the fish swimming a few inches below the surface. The pickup and takeout are as graceful as they are deadly for the fish that now wriggles in his talons.

At that moment, Solix and Ace squawk for the first time since starting their hunt. But Solix signals Ace to quiet down for there is more hunting to do. In an instant, Solix catches a glimpse of geese foraging at the edge of the riverbank. Thinking this is such good luck, he immediately flies beyond the cliff, moving further downstream without being detected. He marks in memory a tree at the edge of the cliff, directly above the geese. When he nears the tree mark, he makes a hard right barrel roll over the edge of the cliff, straightening out into a power dive that sends panic through the flock, one of whom happens to see him diving like a javelin from the sky.

The geese scatter in all directions away from the narrow sandbar at the base of the cliff. Solix is at a tremendous advantage, holding the high ground, able to dive much faster than they can fly. The size of the flock and their confusion below do not bother him one bit, because he targeted his intended meal as soon as he first caught sight of the geese. It's almost as though every other goose could have just stayed put. But of course, no goose knows which one was targeted. So, each one blasts off in its race for life. Running across the water, flapping furiously, zigzagging, darting, flipping feathers and squawking loudly, the geese make so much noise that Ace knows what Solix is up to. Then, as quickly as it started, the hunt ends in mid-air as Solix catches, spears and dispatches his prey in an explosion of flying feathers. Now the other geese are quiet, and Solix is the one squawking loudly, to express his joy at the successful hunt and to let Ace know that more fuel in on the way.

Unknown to him, Solix has just demonstrated another benefit of his partnership with Ace. He doesn't usually perform such aerial attacks, or hunt for geese. His typical prey is earthbound. But he has learned well the art of aerial engagement from Ace. With just one observation of a behavior, he has modified it to suit his own purposes. His innate abilities also figured in this hunt. His ultra-sensitive hearing allowed him to sense the geese from afar. Their presence was not masked, even by the thundering roar of the waterfall. And his sense of distance is enabled by binocular vision and sonarlike echo-location skills. He is one amazing bird!

He flies back upriver to find Ace. Sighting him on the riverbank, he delivers another takeout item for their lunch. By now, Ace has split the fish into two equal parts, one for himself and one for Solix. As he lands with his quarry, Solix begins the chefly task of plucking the goose and making half available to Ace.

"Excellent takeout, if you ask me," says Ace.

"I couldn't agree more. I took it out of the air and you took it out of the water. This is a delicious lunch, and both of our menu choices are perfect fuel for our long journey."

"Yes, we're lucky." confides Ace.

"That's true, but I was referring to the exceedingly high octane of the fuel."

Ace continues, "One of the reasons I like salmon so much, especially this time of year, is that pound for pound it contains more fat than anything else I hunt. The goose was also plump."

"We shouldn't have to eat again for a while," says Solix as he finishes his two-course gourmet dinner.

They both begin to preen their feathers, passing each of them through their beaks to coat them with grooming oil. The process could take quite some time because each has thousands of feathers. However, focusing on the primary flight feathers on each of his wings and on the broader and more symmetric feathers in a tail that unfolds into an exquisite fan, they make short work of this daily task. As they groom, small talk ensues.

Ace questions, "What are you smiling about?"

"Well, Ace, I was just thinking what great partners we make. This last hour has demonstrated several reasons. First, we took advantage of our diverse skills to ensure a successful hunt. Second, we made decisions based on our different tastes, which resulted in a two-course meal that was better than what either of us could have acquired alone."

"Well, there is one serious downside to our partnership: now that I have eaten half a large fish and half a goose, I don't think this Eagle can fly on Friday or any other day soon, unless you can be my tow plane to the nearest thermal!"

"Well, my only comment is that it's not a defect of our partnership but a consequence of your overeating. Besides, with your broad, eight-foot wingspan, it shouldn't take that much effort to reach gliding altitude."

After a brief interlude, they are back on the wing. First climbing above the river, then above the cliff, they easily catch an updraft. Soon neither is flapping his wings any more as they both catch the hoped-for thermal that sends them higher and higher towards the cumulus clouds above. Then they level off into a cruising glide powered by the wind blowing out of the northeast. Soon, however, the wind shifts as they come closer to the clouds. They begin to see lightning and then hear thunder. By now the winds have shifted to such a degree that they are now out of the north, then the northwest.

It is not long before Solix and Ace are being buffeted by increasingly high gusts. This does not bother Ace one bit. He is humming along like a jumbo jet, using the wind to fly faster and save his energy, his fuel. Before they really notice, the wind shifts so much that it is blowing out of the west and they are heading due east. Since they are flying over new territory, they have no ground-based landmarks to signal their position. But soon Solix becomes alarmed as he realizes that they are not traveling south.

Another of his unique capabilities manifests itself: he is able to use the earth's magnetic fields as aids to navigation. He is thrilled by the effortless joy of the wind-driven ride. As a result, he has failed to heed the directional warning indicators going off in his brain. But now, the off-course alarm causes his brain to pulsate. Ace soon receives a similar alarm.

Before course corrections can even begin, rain starts to fall. First it is gentle and soothing. Then, in a steamy flash, it gets heavier, and heavier, until they are flying in near blackout conditions. Another bolt of lightning flashes, heating up the air so much that they both break into a sweat. But no feathers are singed—yet. They are rightly concerned, and scared. Just then, near-panic erupts in them as small hailstones begin hitting them from below, not from above, as they have experienced closer to the ground. Icing on their wings is now a serious threat. At their altitude the air is very cold, and the hail from below signals that temperatures are even colder at lower altitudes. It also tells them that the air is increasingly turbulent. Unless they are extremely careful, their wings will become iced over, and they will become flying ice blocks. Without hesitation, they choose a solution quickly.

Solix retracts his wings from the broad outstretched configuration of a glider (which exposes the greatest amount of wing surface) to the tucked wing configuration of a delta fighter. His action results in a transition from gliding to diving. Ace follows suit. Soon they are both diving toward a lower altitude at such speeds that they are almost as dry as if they were flying between or around the raindrops. In minutes they are out of imminent danger, but unbeknownst to them, woefully further off-course.

Presto! They are at a comfortable lower altitude where the rain is lighter and the air warmer. Wispy ground fog rises from the mountains below, obscuring their view of the landscape. When they reach a clearing in the sky, they see that there are no trees on the giant mountain peaks below. Soon they see a great emerald lake nestled between two high mountains, sitting as though in a bowl held in enormous stone wings pointing toward the sky. The water of the lake is a shimmering blue–green, caused by the rock flour flowing with the glacial run-off from the surrounding mountains. At the southern end of the lake is a stand of larch, maple, red cedar and Hemlock.

Dejected and soggy, Solix and Ace land near a red cedar not far from the shore. Shaking their entire bodies, in their version of spin dry, they spray water droplets in every direction. Soon they are very dry, aided in the process by the grooming oil coating their feathers. They are now standing closer to the red cedar tree, using its cover as a large umbrella.

"Where are we?" asks Solix.

"I was about to ask you the same thing. I can only tell you that judging by the surroundings, we are not where we want to be!"

"How do you know that?" asks Solix.

"I remember my family talking about the far south range of their territory. The story is that we should fly over a northern rain forest. There should be huge towering Douglas fir and even bigger and taller sequoia. But I haven't seen any of those around here. The mountain ranges should be to our left."

Solix exclaims, "Are we lost?"

"I'm not sure, my friend. The shifting winds and the thunderstorm may have driven us far off course."

"Yes, I'm sure the thunder storm didn't help matters. Ace, I think that in our haste to escape being barbecued, perhaps we took a wrong turn."

"Friend, I think we have just been blown way off course by the fast high altitude winds, and the thunderstorms just compounded our problems." Ace sighs as he continues, "But here we are safe and sound. In the morning, we'll scout the area and figure out where we are." Just then, they hear the chirping of crickets and the retiring songs of grouse. On these notes, the friends settle in to roost for the night in the sheltering red cedar.

6. Natural Aviators

The sunrise is one of the most spectacular that Solix and Ace have ever seen. They emerge from their roosts to begin scouting the area. Breakfast is also high on their list of priorities as they fly a short distance from the red cedar to a rock outcropping at the edge of the lake.

"How do you want to tackle this? Have you looked at those tall mountains? Even though we're on the ground, I feel like I'm at ten thousand feet."

"Yes, I know," responds Solix. "Yesterday we never flew more than twelve sequoias above the ground, but now I have to breathe very deeply and that's unusual for me. Usually, I hardly take more breaths when flying at my fastest than when I am perched on a limb. Just the short flight over here from the red cedar has me panting."

Ace says as he directs, "Then we have to make sure that we have a good plan for scouting this area. We want to gather as much information as we can with the least amount of effort. I propose that you focus on terra firma and I'll explore terra aqua. We need to figure out where we are and how far off course we are."

They agree on Ace's reconnaissance plan and each flies off.

Ace surveys the Emerald Lake first, which he finds very murky because of the rock flour. Unable to see more that a few inches below the surface, he decides to look for ripples in the water that will show him where fish are swimming. Before long, he sees big ripples not far from the shoreline. He hastens to the location for a closer inspection. What he sees are fish that he recognizes as related to his favorite food. But these fish are a different color than he has ever seen before. The first one he sees is covered with the speckled colors of the rainbow. The second one is the muted brown of the fertile earth. He decides that both must be cousins of the salmon. He periodically reminds himself that his mission now is to gather information,

not fish. But it is very tempting to deviate from his self-appointed task. At this point, he decides, "I will keep my promise to Solix and focus solely on the mission."

He flies further, following the water's flow to a point where it exits the emerald-colored lake. The flow forms a small creek, having started as trickles from the glacier far above in the mountains. After a short distance, the small creek is joined by other creeks which began their journeys as glacial run-off from other mountains. The flow of water increases rapidly in speed and volume. Following the emerging river, Ace scouts for more signs of fish and other food sources.

Meanwhile, Solix flies high above the trees, searching for signs of life. In a matter of minutes, he sees dark animals on the black and dark gray rocks far below at the end of the lake opposite the creek. At first glance, he thinks it's strange that all the animals are the same color as the rocks. Closer to the rocks on the mountain, he finds the animals are not moving at all. Even when he swoops down to within inches of what appears to be a vole, it does not flinch. He lands near another animal for an even closer inspection and is amazed to find that animal and stone are one: the animals are cast into the stone. He pecks the animal just to satisfy himself that this isn't highly perfected camouflage. Seeing no movement whatever, he is puzzled and thinks, "We certainly can't eat this! I can't wait to tell Ace about the stone animals," and then, "I'd better not stay here any longer or I may turn into stone myself." At that, he takes a mighty leap skyward, making sure he flies away from this area as fast as his wings will carry him. As he rockets away, he says, "I hope there is better quarry around here than I found in this quarry."

Down the mountain, in a beautiful valley, he sees a village not too far from a small river. He swoops down to a larch forest nearby, alighting on a tree limb with a clear view of the center of the village. He decides that a good way to gather information is to observe these people, who he believes are natives of the area. He sees them coming and going, pursuing various activities that he has seen humans in Wasukeki doing. But he notices that these people are different. They are taller and slimmer than the Inuit he knows. He also notices that the nests they live in are covered with animal skins and shaped like pinecones standing upright on the ground. The native people in the Wasukeki region live in shelters made from ice and compacted snow that looks like pinecones lying flat on the ground and half buried in the snow.

A group of natives is gathering at the edge of the village. Solix sees them hopping up and thinks, "They are moving about like I do sometimes when I am about to go hunt." Curious, Solix quietly repositions himself in another tree so he can get a better look and hear more. What he hears and sees is astonishing: the natives are raising wooden animals toward the sky and chanting songs and beating drums to pace their dancing. These people are new to Solix, and so are the words they speak. He listens intently and manages to remember some of the words spoken as each wooden animal is raised toward the sky: *niska, kinosew, wapos, ankwacas, ocikomsis*, and long words that he only remembers as *paskwa* and *wawas*. Then the natives' mood changes from happiness to caution. They ask the spirits to protect them from the *mahihkan* and *maskwa*, whom they praise as mighty beast equaled only by themselves.

Solix is puzzled by all the words the natives are using, but tries to remember as many as he can. Only much later will he learn that the natives have been asking the animal spirits to be kind to them and to allow them to catch animals so they may feed their children and families.

Pointing toward one of the standing cone nests, one of the natives hands the wooden animals to a beautiful maiden, and says, "wigwam." Just then the drums stop and the dancing halts. The natives pick up other wooden objects and begin walking toward the forest. Solix silently follows at a safe distance, partly because he doesn't know if he is being hunted.

After a half-day trek through the forest, through rivers that run eastward and through meadows, the natives are blessed with an amazing bounty of food. Now heading back toward the village, they have collected only what is needed for their survival. It is only at this point that Solix thinks of Ace. He looks in the direction of the sun and knows that he has been gone a long time. He wonders if Ace has made it back to the red cedar.

In fact, Ace has, and has been waiting for Solix for several hours. Ace caught a nice sized fish in the river that runs westward and brought it back to the red cedar to share with Solix. He is worried that his friend may have found a beautiful maiden of his kind and deserted him. At the precise moment that Solix thinks of him, Ace begins eating half the fish.

Meanwhile, the natives are entering the village. They sing gleefully, so loudly that even Ace can hear their songs echoing off the mountains. They have placed their entire quarry in the center of a grassy area at the edge of the village. One by one they point to each animal as they celebrate: *niska*, *kinosew*, *wapos*, *ankwacas*, *ocikomsis*, *paskwawimostos* and *wawaskesiw*. Finally, Solix knows that these words mean goose, fish, rabbit, squirrel, raccoon, buffalo and elk, each of which has blessed the tribe. Now the tribe is giving thanks to the animal spirits who have granted their request. In doing so, they move their hands to indicate the expanse of the surrounding land (which they call *Yoho*), the earth, and the heavens. They raise their hands to show their appreciation to the Gods. Later Solix learns that in their tongue, *Yoho* means "amazing," as in "amazingly beautiful" and "amazingly bountiful".

As one native hunter walks towards a wigwam, he passes a horse, which kicks him. Solix thinks that perhaps the horse feels he has not been properly thanked for the ride he provided to the hunter. But everyone who passes near the horse is also given a swift kick. Solix decides he will remember this place as the village at Kicking Horse River.

By now, it is almost nightfall. The sun is casting long shadows and Solix panics as he remembers he has not caught a single bit of food for himself and Ace. He expresses his displeasure with a surprised hoot. The indigenous people hear this and turn in the direction of the sound. "Oho!" they say, "oho!" Upon seeing the great bird, they start playing the drums again and dancing, pleased to be blessed by the visit to their village of the great Oho, whose family they hold in great esteem. To show this respect they also bring offerings to the base of the tree in which Solix is perched. Knowing now that they mean him no harm, he remains calm as they approach. A hunter places two rabbits at the base of the tree and says, "Wapo, pika." The natives then leave as the sun sets.

Arriving back at the red cedar, Solix places the two rabbits next to the half-eaten fish as Ace asks, "Where have you been? Did you find a beautiful maiden too?"

"No, no," say Solix. "I found something much better!" He then excitedly tells Ace the story of his day. For hours into the night, far past Ace's normal bedtime, Solix talks about what he has learned. When Ace protests that they should get some sleep, Solix reminds him, "You know I should have been sleeping all day today!" Ace grows excited as he learns what Solix has seen. Because of their enthusiasm, they both fall fast asleep with the two rabbits and half a fish lying nearby, still uneaten.

The following morning, they wake to the echoes of natives' songs from the valley. Since Solix did not eat the day before, he is famished. He says to Ace, "Let's have something to eat. I brought a *wapo* and a *pika* for us."

"They look like rabbits to me," says Ace.

"Well, yes, they are," responds Solix. "The larger one is the *wapo* and smaller one is the *pika*."

"Which one do you want?" Solix asks as Ace brings over the remaining half of fish. "Well, remember we have the fish that I caught, and to be fair, you deserve a share for yesterday and today."

"You're right," exclaims Solix. "I was so excited to learn about the animals in this area that I didn't even eat." They divide the food equally in accordance with their agreement.

During the meal, Solix and Ace continue their conversation from the night before. Comparing notes and seeking clues to their location, they notice the natives' songs are louder and louder, coming closer and closer. They decide to break from their deliberations and see what's going on. By the time they move to the top of the red cedar to get a better view, the natives have reached the base of the tree.

One of the richly dressed men says, *"Pehtam nikamew?"*

Ace asks Solix, "What is he saying?"

"He is asking us if we have heard their singing," responds Solix.

In a desperate attempt to communicate further, the Chief and his people point and sign and mimic to convey their thoughts. In many respects it's comical as speakers of three different tongues try to have a conversation. A native points to himself and says, *"Napew Kakwa."* He then points to the beautiful native maiden and says, *"Iskwew Amo."* Then he points to Ace and says *"Mikisow,"* at which point Ace points to himself and says, "Acaetus." The man points toward the owl and says, "Oho," and Solix points to himself and says, "Solix." They all rejoice that at least they now know each other's names.

As they laugh and smile, another native invites a local Mikisow to join them. Ace and the local Mikisow are able to speak to each other in similar bird languages. With their aid, all proceed to have a more intelligible conversation.

The natives are amazed by Solix because, although they have seen other Oho, they have never seen one his size. For that reason, they continue to pay their respects to him. They are similarly amazed by Ace. When they realize that Solix and Ace come from the Wasukeki region, where they have relatives, they are incredulous. No Oho has ever come here from Wasukeki. No Mikisow or Oho has ever flown to this altitude from the great western coast. When told that the birds are trying to establish new territory further south, the natives advise them to "Follow the Food."

In bidding farewell, Kakwa, Chief of the Tribe at Kicking Horse Valley, further clarifies, "Follow the geese that are marathon flyers but be careful which ones you select." He calls Solix and Ace his brothers and says, "Our people live east of these mountains all the way to the great water."

Drawing a map in the sand to show where some of his people are located, Kakwa also tells them about different geese and their migration routes. Before long the sand is filled with lines: North-South routes radiating from many places in the Arctic, and North-East routes that cross many of the North-South lines. Some lines even run almost due east for hundreds of miles, then Southeast for thousands of miles. Solix and Ace appreciate the respect shown to them by these lessons. But they have absorbed as much of the knowledge as they can in one sitting. By the time they simultaneously say, "We got it, thanks very much," the sand is so filled with lines that they can no longer distinguish which is which.

However, they have learned valuable lessons. They now know that there are numerous families of geese that migrate through this region at this time of year. These geese have spent their summer in the Arctic raising the next generation. They fly south to their winter homes, which are as diverse in location as they themselves are in species.

Ace and Solix have learned that there are four major routes, or flyways, that the migrating birds use: Pacific, Central, Mississippi and Eastern, and that the largest flocks that fly through the area are Canadian Geese, which spend the summer spread across the entire northern part of the continent. Canadian Geese generally fly due south from their summer nesting areas. However, any of these geese may take either flyway. Other facts further complicate the matter, such as that some Canadian Geese do not migrate at all.

In addition, there are many other species of geese with diverse migration routes, who intermix as they fly south. The geese know full well who belongs to each group according to the location of their summer nesting grounds. But if you are not a goose, it is hard to tell which came from where. By following any randomly chosen goose, it is possible to end up anywhere in the region south of Kicking Horse River Valley. As a result, choosing the right geese to follow is key for Solix and Ace.

7. Follow the Food

By this time, the sun is setting once again. Solix and Ace decide to spend another night in the red cedar and to get a fresh start the following morning.

"Ace, let's get a move on!" says Solix. "We learned so much from Kakwa yesterday."

"Yes, and we gathered a lot of information from our scouting trips," responds Ace sleepily. They begin piecing together the complex facts they have heard: Kicking Horse River Valley has lots of fish and game--rainbow fish, earth fish, rabbits, *pikas*, and a variety of other flavorful quarry. Another positive factor is that the natives respect them very much.

Ace says, "I found the rainbow fish in a river that flows to the southwest."

Solix says, "I followed Kakwa and the hunting party along a river that flows to the southeast." With that, they both realize that they are in the place their elders call the Mountains Where the Waters Part, which they were told to keep on their left as they flew south.

"OH, NO, we were not going due south!"

"We were going east or southeast!"

They both exclaim in unplanned unison: "We're east of the great mountains that divide the land! We were told by the elders to stay west of these mountains."

Then they begin to think about how to return to what they now know is the Pacific Flyway. They quickly realize that this will be extremely difficult because of the unusually high winds blowing out of the west. Solix says, "We would have strong head winds all the way."

"What'll we do?" asks Ace. "Winter is coming; the mountain peaks are already covered with a new blanket of heavy snow. We can't stay here for the winter because we're not accustomed to these high altitudes and the coming bitter cold."

Just then Solix looks up to see geese migrating south for the winter. They both know there are several kinds of geese that migrate through this region at this time of year. Pointing skyward, he exclaims, "Let's follow the food! Let's pick the right geese to follow and head south."

At this very moment they stop second-guessing about how they got into this fix and focus on the positive. No more worries about whether the intense Northern lights will interfere with their internal navigation systems. No more anguished thoughts about how they miscalculated the effect of wind and rain on their flight path. No more punishing themselves for using the wind as a natural energy source which left them with fewer options for flight configurations and less ability to control their course.

Now they rejoice in the prospect of leaving Kicking Horse River Valley and celebrating the memory of their elders and the kinship with their new friends. As they continue looking skyward, their decision to follow the geese is manifested in their lift-off. Although they have not yet chosen specific geese to follow, both know that they will just "follow the food."

As they rise above the trees, the natives see them in the sky above their village. They are moved by the birds' apparent appreciation. Tears of joy and reverence flow as they acknowledge the majesty of the birds. The natives thank the geese for visiting Kicking Horse Valley and adding to the abundance in their lives. Kakwa pays the ultimate tribute by saying in his language, "Soar like an eagle, be wise like an owl, and feed your friends like the geese." It is clear that these birds have been held in great esteem for centuries and are an integral part of the culture, symbols of all that is good.

Solix and Ace acknowledge their respect by tipping their wings, meanwhile observing flocks of geese in the distance to the southeast. They shout, "Follow the food!" in gleeful appreciation for the experience they have had and the knowledge they have acquired.

Now flying unnoticed above and behind the migrating flocks, they both know that they face a major decision. Looking at them, Solix and Ace wonder how to choose the right geese to lead them. But for now they focus on the joy of life and the support of their elders and friends.

After some hesitation, they discuss the geese as they cruise almost effortlessly on thermals and winds, always keeping the geese in sight. Even though they are caught up in the excitement of travel, they carefully monitor flight conditions.

As the geese begin to scatter in different directions, following routes known only to themselves, Solix and Ace know this is a critical point. As the routes separate, they have little time left to make their choice. Though they have gained a lot of knowledge from Kakwa and his people, they also realize this knowledge is limited. Among all the V-shaped flight groups below them, at least one is surely going to a place they would like, but which one? At this point, there is no way for them to know and no one to ask.

Remembering Kakwa's map and recalling that all flyways through the Kicking Horse Valley lead south or southeast, Solix says, "Whichever flock we pick, we'll surely end up in the south, most likely in the southwest."

Ace adds, "We've never been to either place so we don't have a basis for choosing, do we?"

"Well, let's think about that." replies Solix. "Kakwa said his people in the southeast are great fishermen. That means there are surely fish there. No details were given about the southwest. So, let's follow the food heading southeast."

Making a calculated guess, based on the general direction that certain V-shaped flight groups have been flying for the past hours, Solix and Ace mark in memory the geese they have jointly determined to be heading southeast.

After hours on wing, Solix says, "Well, I believe we made at least one right choice: these are not local commuters!"

To which Ace replies, "Long distance, marathon fliers. Hooray for the geese that are leading us!"

"Yes, we should thank them for that, as well as for the dinner they'll provide." says Solix.

"Well, Solix, that brings up another key decision, doesn't it? Which goose should we invite to dinner?"

"I agree," replies Solix. "There are a few simple rules. The first is that we should never pick the leader of the flight formation. The second rule is to pick a flight group that is undisciplined, uncoordinated and not flying in a perfect V. The third rule is to pick a goose from the rear of the formation."

"And fourth," adds Ace, "is to pick one that tastes good!"

With those rules well understood, Ace arches his wings so that he is catapulted into a diving attack toward the target below. In a flash, his talons have extended and delivered the dinner invitation.

Solix then quickly follows so that they may land, have a quick dinner and get back on wing. Continuing their sturdy flight, hour after hour, the marathon geese never miss a beat. But Solix and Ace don't worry about losing the geese because they can hear them from miles away. Even so, Ace has an anxious expression on his brow as he looks in their direction.

"Don't worry," says Solix. "at some point they'll need to stop for water or food themselves."

Actually, however, that formation just keeps flying. Hour after hour, day and night, they are the true marathoners of the sky. Luckily for Solix and Ace, more formations appear overhead. So they decide to rest for the night and resume their journey in the morning.

At the break of dawn, they pick out another flock, at random, to follow. These geese are heading in a more easterly direction, but Solix and Ace don't mind.

8. Arrival at Blue Mountain

After a few days of following the food, Solix and Ace find themselves riding on high altitude thermals, followed by long distance glides across a seemingly endless landscape. Then they see a line of mountains in the distance, not nearly as high as the ones they left behind, but beautiful. Recognizing some of the rock formations described by Kakwa in his sand map, Solix says, "The land of our eastern brothers is below. These are the Blue Mountains."

They have crossed the continent in a few days. If such records were kept, they would surely have earned flying crowns. Seeking the right combination of terrain and game to suit both of them, they proceed to explore the landscape. Soon they find that Blue Mountain is prime real estate. Rolling foothills to the East are like giant steps leading to higher ridges and peaks. The western slopes rise gently across high meadows to hilly plains.

Trees of all kinds blanket the landscape, evergreens for winter shelter and hardwoods for nuts, which Solix and Ace don't actually eat, but some of their favorite quarries get fat on them. And there are also trees heavy with fruit, and berry bushes, many of which they do eat.

Ace spots a swift river in a spectacular valley, with sheer rock cliffs, whitewater rapids and calm pools. From their perspective, it looks like a country estate, suitable for both of them. Solix chooses the Hemlock forest for his home. Ace chooses the valley where the swift river runs.

Solix flies for joy, and Ace exclaims, "Wohoo! What a Wonder!" In a final whirling celebration flight, they do a signature paired 'Acesolix' sky dive. As the two rise on a thermal to more than four thousand feet above the peak, Blue Mountain residents can't help but notice. They all gather in the meadow for an unobstructed view. Just then Solix and Ace level off into an easy, gentle glide. Visible only as specks in the sky by even the best visioned member of the crowd below, Ace says to Solix, "How about it? Want one last thrill before we get to work on our new homes?"

"Yes, I'm game. I'm IN," says Solix, focusing on the prospect of a death-defying dive. Silently he checks their strategy to avoid splattering on the beautiful scenery far below. Air is thinner way up here, and dives are faster and more risky, especially with wings covered with ice.

Ace says, "We can't think about this for too long! We can't stay long at this altitude in these conditions." Though their lungs are specially developed to extract oxygen efficiently, they are most concerned about maintaining lift as the thermal current cools down. On Ace's command, both curve their wings downward and backward, better aerodynamically configured than billon-dollar fighters. Ace, and then Solix, drops into a power dive as though jet-powered. This surpasses the sensation of any drop off the highest, steepest roller coaster ever built. To those on the ground, they appear to be accelerating at more than 22 feet per second, from zero to 60 MPH-- less time than a Corvette-- from zero to 90 MPH-- less time than a Ferrari-- and soon they are flying faster than an F-16 on a bombing run. The friends look at each other as Blue Mountain becomes larger and larger, and trees that seemed smaller than match sticks at the beginning of the dive are now clearly ten feet in diameter, two hundred feet in height.

Solix exclaims, "Careful! If we hit those trees, we will surely be doomed!" Both wonder, "Are we at our limits? Have we exceeded the pull-out speed?" They know that attempting to pull out of the dive at too high a speed will surely break their wings, or at least cause them to lose primary wing feathers. Suddenly each looks at the other.

"NOW! NOW! Pull out on Two!" says Ace. "One, Two!" he says in quick cadence, almost as one word. Quickly they create drag by extending their feet away from their bodies. Both strain to carefully contour their wings while angling them backward. They must counteract the tendency to forward somersault in a continuing rapid vertical descent. These are harrowing moments: one wrong move, a foot too far, a wing too stretched out, and they are both done for. Feathers will fly, for sure, each one flying on its own because it will no longer be attached to either body. Indeed, this will be their last hurrah if they hit the trees or Blue Mountain itself at such a speed.

Their closeness to one another at this speed creates another hazard, tremendous turbulence. Both feeling the effects, they fly apart to gain more room to execute the final critical maneuvers. Decelerating now, they must really put on the brakes, as the ground is fast approaching. Wings are brought forward and feet are tucked in. The tendency to somersault cancelled, Solix and Ace are now fighting with all their strength to bring their wings fully forward and outstretched with sufficient flatness to avoid being broken by the wind resistance created by their still high speed. Feathers on both are fluffing and frilling from air turbulence. Some feathers are actually plucked out, filling the air with downy plumage. But primary wing feathers all stay attached, as Solix momentarily thinks of the pain and embarrassment of losing them. Downy feathers, he can explain, were shed because of the heat created by such a fireball flight. But loss of primary feathers would be a huge liability, and unexplainable. But all's well, no need to worry any more. Each has pulled out of the fastest dive ever executed by a living bird.

Sure, they both know birds who have flown or dropped faster, but none are around anymore to talk about it. *They*, however, on the other wing, have approached the avian speed barrier and lived to talk about it. They whoop and holler as they glide toward a landing on Blue Mountain. Below, the assembled crowd gawks in amazement and relief, now knowing that the amazing sky dive will not terminate in a piercing invitation to dinner. The crowd of local residents applauds even more loudly and even breaks out in loud cheers of appreciation until they realize: "Who are we cheering for here?" says one wise citizen. "The ones who were not skewered by powerful talons, or the ones still circling above us?" Nonetheless, they are joyful to have witnessed such an aerial spectacle.

As they exited their dives Solix and Ace were separated by several hundred feet. Each continues on, as though this was the flight plan, toward their chosen home sites. Flying on broad, fully extended wings, they are now ready to settle on Blue Mountain. Solix flies to the Hemlock forest, observing his new neighbors as they break from the open meadow in all directions leading to cover. Many live near Solix's new home: fox, rabbit, woodchuck, and bluejay. The first three have dens in different places on the mountain. The bluejay has a cozy nest of grass high in a silver maple tree. Others live near Ace's new home overlooking the swift river. Frogs have a comfortable place among the bulrushes near the pool at the river's edge. A raccoon has a home in the hollow at the base of a giant oak tree that must be centuries old. They all watch from the safety of their homes to see where Solix and Ace are headed. Solix lands on a Hemlock at the edge of a small clearing several yards from the meadow, and Ace on a towering pine with a hefty forked limb outstretched over the swift river. Solix hoots as if to say, "Perfect, perfecto, excellent" all in a singing melody.

Ace hears and replies, "Perfect, perfecto, excellent" in harmony with his friend's echo.

They separately go about the work of building their homes. For Solix it's a simple matter of scratching out a depression in the end of a snag Hemlock. For Ace it's even simpler; he needs only a good perch since a nest is needed only if one has a mate. Of course, it's much too early for that, since they arrived only today. Even so, Ace can't help but rejoice over his good fortune.

9. Kinships

Solix is awakened the next morning by chatter not far from his new home. A woodchuck and rabbit are having an animated discussion. Their voices loud and agitated, each appears to be expressing an opposing point of view. Tempers are beginning to flare. This ruckus has awakened Solix, who is quite disturbed. He had intended to catch up on his rest after his journey. This quarrel has derailed his plans. Angry at being disturbed, he leaves the Hemlock to investigate the source of the unintended alarm clock.

Soon, he locates the site of the argument. He silently perches, unnoticed, on a limb of a dogwood near the commotion, listening intently. He knows the languages of the woodchuck and rabbit because for thousands of generations members of their families have regularly been dinner for his family.

As it turns out, they are arguing about whether the new owl is someone that they know. It is apparent to Solix that they think he is a former friend. He is at first confused by this possibility, then curious as to how it could be possible. Deciding to discuss the matter with his neighbors, and careful not to alarm either, Solix again uses stealth to fly down to a position a few feet behind them. When they notice, they are startled and he hastens to say, "Don't worry. I mean you no harm. You woke me up with your argument."

The woodchuck and rabbit move away cautiously as each apologizes for any inconvenience caused.

"What," may I ask "are you arguing about?"

"Well," says the woodchuck, "residents in these parts have always heard the legend of Solomon Owl. He was a highly respected individual in these parts. But this was a very long time ago. According to the legend, Solomon Owl moved away from Blue Mountain without telling anyone where he was going. For years, the locals hoped he would return but he never did. Now you are here and this silly rabbit thinks that you are the returning

Solomon Owl. Of course, that would be impossible, because according to the legend, Solomon Owl left Blue Mountain about eighty-eight years ago. That would mean that his one-hundredth birthday is this year. I told the silly rabbit that owls don't live *that long* and that if you were Solomon Owl you would be unable to fly so fast, and you certainly wouldn't look as young as you do.   I also reminded her that it would be impossible for a hundred-year-old owl to put on the aerial display that you did yesterday. Indeed, no hundred-year-old owl would be stupid enough to try that."

At that point, the rabbit jumps further out of reach, fearing that the new owl will take offense at the woodchuck's comments and attack both of them. Quite the contrary: Solix begins to laugh, so much that his stomach hurts. Tensions are substantially reduced by this turn of events. The rabbit apologizes, "Sorry we've been so rude. May I introduce myself? I am Jagus S. Obscur, and this is Pochata M. Monax."

"Pleased to meet both of you. I am Solix Strix Nebul; I am from the Wasukeki region, which is far, far to the northwest. I have come here to establish a new home for myself and a new territory for my family."

Pochata glanced over her shoulder to see other approaching forest inhabitants.   The early morning debate has attracted several curious onlookers, who have gathered to learn what the commotion was all about and perhaps to join the argument. As they move closer, Pochata glances again to see new instigators moving toward the front of the advancing crowd. Now all are anxious to hear what Solix has to say.

"Well," he continues, "I can easily settle your dispute because I am certainly only four years old."

"That may be," says Jagus, "but Solomon Owl has returned, because his spirit lives in you."

With that statement, Pochata does not disagree, for it is clear to her that Solix is of the same family as Solomon Owl.

"Who are your families?" asks Solix.

Pochata responds, "Our families have been residents of this area for centuries. I am a descendant of Polly Woodchuck, who was a friend of Solomon Owl, and Jagus is a descendant of Jimmy Rabbit, who was also his friend."

Jagus adds, "The descriptions I have heard of Solomon Owl fit you perfectly. Could it be that you are one of his descendants?"

"That's hard to know," says Solix. "My elders have never told me about a Solomon Owl or about this place, which my friend and I call Blue Mountain."

"Blue Mountain!" exclaims Jagus. "How do you know the name of our mountain? As I told Pochata, you *must* be Solomon because you wouldn't know the name of our valley unless you had been here before."

"No, no," says Solix. "It's not that way at all. We called this place Blue Mountain because when we first saw it from miles away, it looked like it was shrouded in these low clouds that in our eyes looked blue."

Pochata introduces Solix and tells the assembled forest dwellers that he is a descendant of Solomon, or at least is from the same extended family. The fox, who is now on the scene, says, "I'm a descendant of Tommy Fox. My name is Tomes V. Vulpes. I'm pleased to meet you."

Yet another resident appears and joins the conversation, interjecting, "I am Faton P. Lotor, and I am a member of the raccoon family that has lived on this mountain for many, many generations."

In fact, Solix meets a large number of residents who know the legend of Solomon Owl. The families differ in size. For example, Solix is told that there are no other descendants of Solomon Owl anywhere on Blue Mountain. On the other hand, everywhere he looks he sees relatives of Jagus, but notes fewer relatives of Pochata.

Solix wonders, "Why is it that there are none of my family still here on Blue Mountain? Even if Solomon Owl left the mountain, wouldn't he have had fledglings who stayed? Why would they all have left the mountain?" He is perplexed and has no answers to his own questions. Nor do the other residents. After much discussion about their ancestors, they

realize that a large number of generations have come and gone since the days of Solomon Owl, in the case of Solix, twenty-two. Tomes represents the thirty-third generation of his family, and Pochata is a forty-fourth-generation descendant of Polly, while Jagus is an eighty-eighth-generation descendant of Jimmy.

The residents begin to tell stories about Solomon Owl and their ancestors. Solix listens intently, very interested in his family's history. His curiosity is especially piqued by the continual references to Solomon Owl, who he believes must have been an impressive bird. He listens as Tomes tells how Solomon Owl first arrived on Blue Mountain.

"Let me tell you about him. Long ago, there was this farmer who owned a farm in the valley. He was always afraid of Solomon Owl because his hoots were so piercing. Solomon was not a menace to the farmer and only occasionally was he a menace to his chickens. From time to time Solomon would take a chicken or two for dinner. This made the farmer very mad. But he failed to appreciate Solomon's work catching voles by the hundreds each year. In truth, the farmer came out far ahead. Evidently he did not realize this, because he still wanted to get rid of Solomon. A feud erupted between them, and Solomon wanted the farmer to leave the valley as much as the farmer wished Solomon would go away."

"That's an interesting story," says Solix "Why did Solomon Owl think it would be a good thing for the farmer to leave the valley? Did that have anything to do with why Solomon Owl left?" None of the residents knows the answer. Solix continues, "Why didn't the farmer like Solomon Owl? Didn't he benefit from Solomon's expert hunting?" Again there is silence from the residents.

Solix becomes concerned that his family was banished from Blue Mountain years ago by the farmer. Does this mean that he himself will be in danger here? He is alarmed by the prospect of reopening an old feud. He wants to live a peaceful existence, without conflict with man or beast.

10. New Challenges

As Solix ponders these questions, his buddy arrives in the meadow and sees the gathering. Solix motions for him to come over and says, "May I introduce my partner, Ace? We made the journey together from the far northwest region."

Ace begins to tell about their epic journey across the continent, from the great northwest across the great western mountains and over the Great Plains, to reach Blue Mountain. The tale takes hours, but all the residents listen patiently and with great interest. Ace puts lots of emphasis on the challenges that they faced and how they worked together to overcome them.

Solix is intrigued that his ancestors lived on Blue Mountain but is puzzled about why they left, never to return for 88 years. He looks to Tomes for answers and insight.

Tomes says, "Solomon was well liked by the residents of Blue Mountain but they were also wary of him. At times they tried to drive him out of his house."

"Maybe that's why he left Blue Mountain," says Solix. Worrying that his own presence on Blue Mountain may be at risk, he feels it is important to understand the reasons why Solomon left Blue Mountain so long ago. If people didn't want him around here, they may not want Solix, either. In that case, he would not be happy here. More disappointingly, he would have to look further for a suitable territory.

He is pleased with his Blue Mountain home, believing the setting is perfect for him. There is an open meadow with grasses, bushes and rock outcroppings that make a perfect home for voles. There is a stream that runs through the meadow, empties into Swift River a mile away, and provides shelter for the frogs that are another staple of his diet. There are beautiful flowers dotting the landscape that attract a variety of insects on which birds feed. The meadow is therefore a natural attractant for all the kinds of birds that Solix favors from time to time. Rabbits and squirrels are abundant in the meadow and surrounding woods. Hemlock, pine and oak trees form a forest canopy that shields the mountain. As he surveys this scenery, he is convinced that Blue Mountain is the perfect home for him. But he still can't help wondering why his ancestors left so long ago. Is this a bad omen for him and his life here?

He ponders whether there are other Nebulosa nearby. Could some of the descendants of Solomon be living in other parts of the Blue Mountain Range? If so, why haven't they visited the Swift River area in so long? Seeking answers from the local residents, he is told that they are positive that none of Solomon's family has been to Swift River in eighty-eight years. They also tell him that other animal populations on Blue Mountain have been decimated.

During the past twenty years, he is told, the frog population has declined significantly. Since frogs are another of his favorite foods, he is especially concerned. None of the residents can explain the devastating loss of the frog community. Every kind of frog has been affected: the bullfrogs, their neighbors in the stream, which croak during the day, and the tree frogs, which croak at dusk and into the night. Tomes says, "They made such melodic music they were an essential part of our community."

Everybody agrees that certain foods are critical to their survival and that they should all be concerned when their neighbors leave. Solix remembers the issues in the Wasukeki region and the food crisis which caused him and Ace to leave. "Perhaps," he says, "that is why the frogs are no longer on Blue Mountain: their food supplies were shrinking below levels needed to sustain them."

"No," says Tomes. "That alone does not explain it. If that were all, then at least some of the frogs should still be here. There are still many insects around and many water bugs in the stream."

"It's another great mystery," says Solix. "What could be causing the imbalance here? In the Wasukeki region, the food crisis was the result of a warm early spring. Could similar climate changes be affecting the frogs here, even though it's thousands of miles away?"

Tomes sighs, "If frog and vole populations fall below critical levels, we will have to leave Blue Mountain just as Solix and Ace left the Wasukeki region. If all the frogs expire, then some of us will certainly pass on with them!"

In spite of this issue, Solix is determined to make Blue Mountain his new home. It is beautiful in so many respects, but there are clearly issues that he will need to address. He decides to expand his hunting range if any prey populations fall below their tipping point. The local residents applaud this decision, but from Solix's perspective it is not entirely altruistic.

Ace, agreeing that they need to keep a keen eye on things so they do not contribute to a food crisis here, is also satisfied with his Blue Mountain home and has not detected any problems yet. The Swift River valley is perfect for him. He has a comfortable perch in the pine tree along its bank. The river is no more than a few feet deep along this stretch, with a rocky bottom filled with many small pebbles, excellent spawning grounds for fish. A few miles downstream from his perch, there is a gigantic waterfall where the river waters cascade over a sheer granite cliff to plunge thunderously hundreds of feet into a multicolored canyon.

In spite of some concerns, Solix and Ace are confident that they have made a good decision in choosing Blue Mountain as their new home. They follow their daily routines, which are generally uneventful, but occasionally they have more excitement than they bargain for.

One exceedingly picturesque fall day, when the leaves of the hardwoods and other deciduous plants form a palette of golden yellow, orange, bronze and seemingly hundreds of other shades, Ace notices leaves floating downriver. Among them is an equally colorful "rainbow fish." Without hesitation, Ace effortlessly sails off his perch toward the river below. The large fish does not appear to have a chance as Ace swoops

down, but it is Ace who is snared as his talons take a penetrating grip. The usual tactic is to spear the fish with his talons, then fly off for a happy meal. But on this day, the catch is not routine. Ace struggles to lift the fish from the water. He flaps his wings furiously to avoid being pulled into the water by the fish's struggles. The fish, wounded but not disabled, thrusts its broad tail, furiously splashing and paddling toward deeper water. Ace is horrified as he tries to resist the fish's stronger and stronger pull. His talons are now fully submerged, as are his legs.

Ace is a strong swimmer and begins to use his wings as oars. Flying is no longer an option since with each attempted wing beat, his feathers become heavier with the soaking spray created by the struggle. The large fish continues dragging him into deeper and deeper water. He knows that the only way to release the fish is to press hard enough to unlock his talons, which have firmly penetrated the fish's flesh. Unfortunately, the river here is too deep for that maneuver. When the fish is pushed into an underwater rock by the rapid current, it is forced upward. Ace feels the upward motion and quickly tries again to lift it from the water. But his efforts prove futile. "I'm doomed!" he cries out, as the roar of the waterfall becomes louder and louder--and he realizes there is no way to release the fish.

He squawks in a shrill, high pitch, perhaps beseeching the fish to swim toward shore in return for its release. Otherwise, he knows both are finished if they are catapulted over the high waterfall.

Solix hears Ace's distressed appeals.

Interrupting his quiet morning in a meadow, Solix streaks off toward Swift River, flying fast and furiously toward the anxious calls. There he sees Ace in the rapids approaching the falls. Without hesitation, Solix accelerates because only seconds remain. Just as Ace and the fish are thrown over the falls like projectiles, Solix harpoons the fish's tail. In a horrific scene, the fate of the three is now inexorably intertwined. Because Solix dove so fast to catch Ace, his downward momentum accelerates their fall toward the jagged rocks below. The two birds are squawking at the top of their voices. Even the fish, an animal not known to produce vocal sounds, contributes to the cacophony echoing off the canyon walls. Even Solix and Ace are startled by the sounds he emits and look him in the eye as if to say, "*You* can squawk? *You* can talk?"

By now the two friends are flapping their wings furiously as the three continue to fall toward the canyon floor. Doused by torrents of waterfall spray, they are fast becoming water-logged in mid-air. Gradually, as their efforts pay off, they come out into spray-free air, finally leveling off and hovering. But navigating between sheer rock cliffs is no easy task. Neither has ever flown in the configuration of a four-blade helicopter before. And their flight control is complicated by the continuing wriggling of the fish. Each of its movements changes their wing pitch, and thus unintentionally sabotages their directional control. Fighting to control the situation, Solix and Ace bend the fish so that they now face each other. His wriggles cease and their wings no longer crash against each other. Working in tandem, the birds finally manage to fly out of the canyon. Local residents are treated to a sight they have never seen before: two birds carrying a single enormous fish, one so heavy that Solix and Ace quickly land along the river's edge just above the falls. Upon landing, Ace's talons automatically unlock and Solix releases his grasp. Seeing the fish is still alive, they take no action as it slips back into the river and heads back upstream. A breathless Tomes scampers onto the scene, expecting a hearty meal. Seeing the fish struggling toward deeper water, at first he tries to pursue it.

"Why did you let that nice, fat fish escape?" he barks at the top of his lungs. Solix and Ace wink as they look at each other.

11. Alliances

Their struggle has brought Solix and Ace to an unfamiliar part of the valley. As Ace contemplates his mortality and good fortune, his friend goes off to investigate. What he sees is quite alarming. In this part of the forest Solix observes thousands of Hemlocks, dead or dying a slow death. Small insects cover the needles of the Hemlocks, and frogs cover the forest floor, also dying but from an unknown cause. Solix approaches one of the trees and sees it covered with what looks like snow. But further inspection reveals that the little white puffs are alive, creating a trail of dripping Hemlock sap. The culprits are billions of little bugs, each smaller than a juniper berry. He smells the sap, which he knows well from when it oozes from the scratches he makes while building a home in a knothole of a snag Hemlock. Here the aroma of the sap, as the bugs devour it, is overpowering. . Solix finds this astonishing, indeed, because this sap is highly toxic and kills almost any living creature. Yet these little insects are eating it like maple syrup! To a Hemlock, sap is its life's blood. Drain away the sap, and you drain life from each tree. With millions of bugs sucking on a single tree, it is apparent that the Hemlocks' defenses are not sufficient to ward off these invaders.

Solix flies further down the mountain and sees that the Hemlocks in the adjoining valley are not covered with the bugs. These trees form neat, long, straight rows between plowed fields of crops. Over the fields he flies, approaching the rows close enough to see that the Hemlocks are not infested. He wonders, "How could this be?" But this question is soon answered as the farmer comes with a tractor, spraying milky water on trees and crops alike. As soon as the spray hits the trees, the white bugs turn a horrid green as they twitch and squirm in an agonizing death. Falling from the Hemlock needles, they form a disgusting carpet surrounding the apparently healthy Hemlock row.

Solix quickly deduces that this spray must be a very powerful poison. If the bugs can eat Hemlock sap like candy with no disabling effect, but are instantly killed by the tractor's milky spray, then it is not something Solix wants to be near. He immediately hightails it back to the safety of Blue Mountain.

Back in the meadow, he is met by Tomes and other animals. He begins talking excitedly and nervously about the Hemlock bugs and his experience near the crops.

"Oh, no!" says Tomes. "You didn't breathe the spray from the farmer's tractor, did you?"

"No," says Solix, "but I saw him spraying the Hemlock row and killing the white bugs."

"You're lucky! I wouldn't wish you such a death," says Tomes as he cautions, "If even a tiny droplet of the farmer's mist gets on you, you will surely die a painful death! Your feathers will crinkle and curl. Your eyes will go dim. Your breathing will become heavy and labored. Your body will shake and shiver as though it were thirty degrees below zero and you were wet but hadn't preened in a year."

Solix shutters at these thoughts. He wants to save the Hemlocks because they have always been a key resource for him. However, he knows that even though the farmer's spray will kill the bugs, it will also kill all the other animals that come in contact with it. Yet the bugs are spreading so rapidly that something must be done quickly.

Tomes suggests that they consult with Pochata.

"What natural repellent can we use to get rid of the bugs on the Hemlocks?" asks Solix.

Pochata responds. "It's an impossible task! I know of herbs that will cause the bugs to become dehydrated and die. Unfortunately, this remedy only works if it is put directly on each bug."

Solix sees the problem, "The bugs are infesting Hemlocks covering more than a million acres. Even if enough of the remedy could be made, how would we put it on all those billions of bugs?"

Tomes suggests, "We have to mobilize the whole community to save our home. If the bugs continue spreading as they have during the past year, soon they will kill all the Hemlocks."

Ace asks, "Who can we enlist to do this monumental job? Who likes eating insects?"

"The perfect candidates are woodpeckers," says Pochata. "Some of them eat insects and some eat tree sap! They should be perfect for this job, if they will agree."

Tomes asks, "Well, what are we waiting for? If the Hemlocks die, it will upset nature's balance all over Blue Mountain and that will affect everyone. Where do we find the woodpeckers? Give me the directions to their home and I will summon them. Solix, you figure out a plan to compensate the woodpeckers for helping to get rid of the bugs."

"Okay, I'll look into that right away," Solix responds. "The woodpeckers can do a lot to control bugs on the trees. Tell them we would greatly appreciate their efforts. We need them to come and peck for a principle!"

There are many more bugs than the local woodpeckers would ever be able to eat. But each bird normally pecks about ten thousand times per day, and so can either consume or peck off that many bugs. Even at that rate, however, a lot of woodpeckers will be needed to do the job.

The variety of bug destroying the Hemlocks does not particularly appeal to all woodpeckers. Those who eat tree sap may not like them, and even the ones who eat insects may not like the taste of these, or tolerate the sap the bugs thrive on. As Ace receives directions and flies off to get the woodpeckers, the discussion continues into the evening.

Solix remembers he has human brothers living somewhere in this region, the fish-people, as Kakwa called them, and he flies off into the moonlit night to find them, aided only by his innate abilities. As he emerges above the forest canopy, he surveys the sky for signs of a native village. Far in the distance, he sees flickering embers rising in the smoke of a campfire. As he gets closer, he sees the fire has been made by a hunting party that has settled down for the night. Cautiously approaching the camp, he notes them using the campfire to smoke fish from a stream feeding into Swift River. The fish are skewered with twigs holding fillets against wooden racks leaning near the several campfires that impart their cedar aroma and caramel color.

Solix lands without a sound on a tree limb overlooking the camp. He observes the natives singing and dancing around the fire. They are clearly celebrating their bountiful harvest. Solix recognizes some of the wooden figures lying on a buckskin blanket. Just then, a native catches a glimpse of Solix's eyes as they reflect the moonlight in two shimmering golden flashes. "Oho," he whispers to another at the campfire. There is a stir of activity and word circulates around the campfire, causing the drumming and singing to cease. "Oho," they all say in unison, as they stand and raise their hands, pointing in the direction of the red oak harboring Solix. "Oho!" they shout as they grow more excited. "Oho!" they acknowledge with praise this good omen. The drumming, singing and dancing resume with such vigor that everyone in the camp is awakened and drawn to the campfire nearest the red oak.

As they approach, Solix hears their repeated chant of "Oho, Oho, Oho," in rhythm with the drums and the stamping feet. Bells and shells clang in syncopated motions to create an accompanying chorus. "Oho, Oho, Oho," they continue as they celebrate the end of an eighty-eight-year absence.

Solix recognizes their chants as they pay respect to him. "*Cherokee*," he says in a hooting greeting. "*Cherokee*, my brothers!" he praises loudly. It is a joyous scene, as if long lost brothers have been reunited. Solix flies down from the red oak toward the approaching tribe. As he circles above the assembly, with both hands a brave raises a spear over his head horizontally. Responding to the signal, Solix lands precisely in the center of the spear between the outstretched hands. As the parade turns toward the camp, more drums sound out a special message heard miles away at the main village. By morning, the small camp is overrun with celebrants. It is a sight to behold! The return of a life from the presumed dead is cause for great rejoicing.

Tsali of the Cherokee tribe arrives and declares this the greatest event since the return of the Ivory-Billed Woodpeckers, which were sighted about two years ago.

Solix feels honored. The Cherokee have been praying for many years for the return of the Nebulosa. They understand why Solomon, the last of his kind to leave the forest, migrated elsewhere. More importantly, they view the return of the Nebulosa as a sign that things on Blue Mountain are, in some respects, improving.

"I have come to ask your help," Solix respectfully announces to Chief Napew, as he tells the tribe about the problems with the Hemlock bugs.

Tsali responds, *"Hemlock wooly adelgid are the new enemies of our forest!"*

Startled, Solix knows immediately that the tribe is aware of the infestation, as they call the insects *"exotic aliens"* and curse their presence in the forest.

Tsali continues, *"These insects will have a catastrophic impact on the forest if we don't do something now!"*

The Hemlocks play a crucial part in the ecology of Blue Mountain. No other plant casts shade as sheltering, no other tree thrives as well in the subdued light beneath the forest canopy, and no other tree covers the steep ravines and banks of rivers and streams, thereby keeping the waters clear. No other tree in the forest has a growth cycle as responsive to shade and sun. Along the banks of rivers and streams, the Hemlock provides a thermostat for the nearby ground and water. Streams that would otherwise freeze over in winter are free-flowing and ice-free all year, enabling the ever-moving rainbow fish and its relatives to thrive. In the Blue Mountain Range there are Hemlocks that first sprouted more than three hundred years before Columbus arrived on these shores.

Solix is overwhelmed by the high praise the Cherokee have for the Hemlock. Never has he seen a people show such admiration for a plant. Chief Napew continues, "Hemlock forests shelter and sustain great numbers and varieties of wildlife. They are less prone to the effects of seasonal droughts and help to abate floods. The Hemlock killed by the wooly adelgid will leave holes in the forest canopy and worsen the effects of ever-increasing temperatures on Blue Mountain. The wooly invaders are destroying our forest home. We must find a way to help the Hemlock."

"Chief Napew," asks Solix. "What are we going to do?"

"The arrival of the Ivory-Billed Woodpecker among the great cypress in the swamps of the Lower River Delta is a very good omen. Now *you* have come to Blue Mountain. We must form an alliance against those miniscule wingless creatures who threaten us. They are immobile for most of their lives as they suck the sap of life out of our Hemlock. We must use a natural remedy: the adelgid will be easy targets for the woodpeckers who are the best among us for this task."

Reassured by these words, Solix is more confident. "We have already summoned them for help!" he replies. By this time, Ace has arrived at the home of the yellow-bellied sapsuckers, the woodpeckers whose aid he seeks. He is led up through the pecking order to Queen Sphyra. After diplomatic greetings, he asks her, "Will you help us get rid of a major pest in the forest?" He appeals further, "We have a situation that you could assist us with: the wooly bugs are killing the Hemlock trees in great numbers. We must defend them against these foreign invaders. I have been sent to seek your assistance. You are very good at pecking. Each of your pecks could eliminate one or more of the bugs. All of you working together could get rid of the invaders."

"In other words, you want us to peck for a principle!" queries Queen Sphyra. "Do you understand that this will cause us to violate another important principle?"

"Which is?" asks Ace.

"Woodpeckers only peck at food to satisfy their hunger. It is not our custom to peck the life out of anything without a good reason."

"We understand that draconian measures are required in these dire circumstances. We do not ask you lightly. The entire forest community is at risk, including your family," says Ace respectfully but with emphasis.

"Peck for a principle! We will use our pecking power to help!" asserts Queen Sphyra, as she commands all of her troops to assemble. She also sends out calls for other woodpeckers, especially those that like to eat insects. She warns that this will be a somewhat unpleasant task for all of them. "None of us have ever eaten these foreign invaders before. They have a waxy, hairy covering that looks as if it will gum up our mouths. They are so small and numerous that it will take millions of pecks to get rid of them all."

12. Commitment

Solix and Ace return to Blue Mountain Meadow and report to the residents. The birds have formed alliances with two key partners, the Cherokee and the Woodpeckers. They have made a commitment to stay and fight for their new homeland, concluding that moving further is not a viable option. The best strategy is to defend the new home that they have come to love. By galvanizing the support of local residents and new allies, Solix and Ace believe they can overcome the menace posed by the foreign invaders.

Solix has pondered the possible reasons why Solomon left Blue Mountain years ago. He may have moved north to avoid conflict with the farmers in the valley, or to find more plentiful food supplies. Whatever his reasons, his departure created a void in the local community, and he is still sorely missed by the residents of Blue Mountain. Solix has a new sense of pride, a heightened sense of responsibility, in re-establishing Solomon's legacy.

The wooly adelgid will not destroy Blue Mountain! The alliance will bring them under control or destroy them all together. They will no longer devour the Hemlock forest.

An ultimatum is sent to the adelgids, "Leave the Hemlock forest or be vanquished from the earth!" Horror and panic spreads among the adelgid. They cannot move in this phase of their lives. They must explain this to the alliance. They do not intend any malice. Their presence here is not of their doing, but is the result of the careless, unintentional actions of others, who brought them from East Asia. It is not their fault that they were brought here from so far away, a journey they could not have made on their own. They have followed a very simple set of laws. Conditions here are ideal for them to multiply, so they have. The normal mortality they would suffer during the winter has been eliminated by the warmer weather throughout the region. And the absence of any natural enemies has contributed to an unimpeded exponential growth in their population, even as a plentiful supply of Hemlock sap has provided the nourishment to support their high birth rate. They simply continue to follow the simple rules of nature and are not to blame for the catastrophe they are creating.

But they do not expect these explanations to assuage the growing concerns of the allies.

And even if the wooly adelgids want to cooperate, they cannot remove their bodies from the Hemlocks. The only way to address the problem is through the intervention of the allies. With the commitment of all concerned, the Alliance springs into action. The Woodpecker troops assemble under the direction of Queen Sphyra, who commands an impressive and formidable regiment.

At her command, the squadron takes wing en route to Swift River Falls, where it has been decided the assault will begin. Within minutes, the queen's troops form a thick, undulating cloud in the sky above Blue Mountain. On their arrival at the rendezvous point, she issues the orders of the day. A platoon of one hundred fifty troops is assigned to each Hemlock. It takes four hours to assign troops to the first five hundred trees. As they begin work, the forest buzzes with activity. Each Hemlock shakes from the pecking of its squad. The woolies are dispatched with such efficiency that each squad finishes a tree a day. The forest floor beneath each cleaned tree is covered with the glum remnants of the pests.

After the first day the troops are exhausted, not by pecking but by their efforts to keep themselves clean as the woolies splatter. It is clear that they cannot continue at this pace. They have the desire, adrenaline and strength, but there are millions of infested Hemlocks in the forest. At this rate they may never overcome the advancing hordes of adelgids.

Solix sees this too and worries about what else can be done. Perhaps the farmer's spray is the only solution, but it would be risky to all the animals of Blue Mountain. Is there a way to spray the bugs without harming the other animals? He thinks, "Perhaps all the animals can evacuate the area until well after the farmers finish. But how long would they have to be

away? Could it be that Solomon left Blue Mountain for similar reasons?" He has more questions than answers as he ponders the grave situation.

He consults with Pochata and Ace to come up with a strategy to assist the Queen and her troops. They all feel helpless standing by as the woodpeckers' bills become gummed with the waxy crusts of the wooly adelgids' outer shells.

Pochata suggests cleaning stations positioned near each tree and manned by the earthbound creatures of the forest, who could use one of her special herbal solutions to clean the woodpeckers' bills. The solution will be made from the juice of two berries with wonderful properties. Not only will it remove the wax and other debris, it will coat the mouths of the woodpeckers with a substance that makes the bitter bugs taste sweet. By the next morning, Pochata and her helpers have whipped up enough batches of this concoction to supply all the necessary cleaning stations. Ace directs the assignment of community residents to scrub and polish the woodpeckers' bills, and they then resume their pecking.

However, everyone is severely alarmed as another problem crops up. With so many woodpeckers working on each Hemlock, their thousands of pecks per tree are wounding the trees. The wooly adelgids are tightly lodged at the base of each needle. At this juncture of needle and bark, the tree is very vulnerable. Each peck is a double-edged sword: a wooly is dispatched, but the host is wounded in the process. With only a few pecks of this sort, the trees would overcome the assault. However, thousands of pecks are inflicted on each tree. If the trees could speak, they would surely moan and cry. If they had a nervous system, they would twitch with pain and anguish as each peck delivers its liberating pierce.

Solix wonders, "Is there nothing we can do to spare them this pain?"

Tsali, who has also been assessing the situation, arrives with important news. The Cherokee, it turns out, have been working with the farmers to find an acceptable solution to the infestation. For years other foreign invaders--gypsy moth and pine bark beetles--have received more

attention because of their devastating impact on the farmers' hardwood and pine plantations. After reclaiming huge tracts of timberland lost to them for centuries by broken treaties, the Cherokee have worked with the farmers to better manage the forest. This cooperation has led to the development of experimental remedies that have been tested in laboratories for years. However, none has ever been field tested because of concerns about their impact on the environment. The Cherokee and the farmers are now considering the use of such a remedy. Should they take this risk? Should they use a weapon whose impact is not yet fully understood? Tsali leans toward avoiding the new remedies. But the farmers want to try them because of their concern for the forests further down the mountain. They fear that at the rate the insects are spreading, it will be a matter of months before they reach their commercial forests. Will their decision create problems worse than those posed by the ravenous bugs?

For Solix and Ace, it is too much to contemplate as they seek refuge in thought about their wonderful journey and their people back in the Wasukeki region. As the geese fly far overhead on their northward migration, Ace daydreams about Halia and hopes silently that one of the geese will recognize him and tell her that he has found a new home on Blue Mountain.

"How will we ever get word to the Wasukeki region that we are here and have new homes on the beautiful Blue Mountain once inhabited by their ancestors?" Solix daydreams as he recognizes one of the flocks above and exclaims loudly, "There are the marathon flyers who led us from the Emerald Lake!"

Ace shouts to him, "The marathon geese are heading north for the summer! Should we follow them again? Do you think they have seen us and will tell Kakwa that we have found our brethren? Do you think they are heading for the Wasukeki region and can tell everyone there about our whereabouts?"

"Ace, you have too many questions I don't have answers for," says Solix as the sun sets. "Let's sleep on it and maybe we'll have better insights in the morning."